/// ALWAYS THE /// BIGOT

/// ALWAYS THE /// BIGOT

James Barclay

LINDSAY
PUBLICATIONS

First published in 2005 by
Lindsay Publications
Glasgow

© James Barclay 2005

ISBN 1 898169.35.7

The moral right of the author has been reserved

British Library Cataloguing-in-Publication Data
A Catalogue record for this book is available
from the British Library

Designed and typeset by Eric Mitchell, Glasgow
and C & R Graphics Cumbernauld

Printed and bound Bell & Bain, Ltd Glasgow

CONTENTS

DEDICATION

This book is dedicated to
Jock Tamson and
ALL
His Bairns

CHAPTER ONE

JEAN UNPLUGGED THE HOOVER, WOUND THE CABLE AND STORED it away. Hands on hips, she stood back and surveyed her handiwork. Yes, her mum would be pleased. Annie Thomson was a stickler for cleanliness and tidiness.

Jean's husband Clarence had dropped her off at her parents' high-rise flat in London Road, so that she could have the place spick and span for her folks arrival from Italy where they had been on holiday. She wondered how Andra, her true-blue dad, had been affected by his trip.

The vacation was the result of a raffle win. The ticket had been purchased by Andra's pal, Hughie Broon who, feeling sorry for a "wee wumman" selling the tickets outside McDougall's pub – Andra and Hughie's favourite hostelry – thought he would give his pal a treat. After all, the first prize was a two-gallon flask of whisky. The second was a trip to a European capital for two. Unfortunately, Andra's ticket had won the second prize and it was off to Italy with a disappointed Andra and an over-the-moon Annie. The "wee wumman" turned out to be a Carmelite nun who, Hughie thought, was a poor wee sowel who worked in a confectionery factory. Andra, a staunch Protestant, was furious at the thought of going to a city that he described as *Hell on Earth*.

Annie his wife, a devout Catholic, was delighted. They had argued non-stop for weeks before the trip. Annie, after lighting two dozen votive candles in the chapel, reinforced by a weekly novena to Saint Jude, patron saint of hopeless cases, had seen Andra capitulate for the sake of peace. He was not pleased! After all, he'd given into his wife's ambitions just a year ago when she wanted to leave their tenement home in Bridgeton and move to the twenty-seventh floor of the new London Road high flats!

Andra was suspicious of his wife's motives. Annie argued it was for the sake of having a bathroom and inside toilet. The flat also had a verandah that she spent many sunny days sitting on in a rocking-chair enjoying the fresh air. *But* the flat overlooked Celtic Park – the football team favoured by Glasgow's Catholic population *and* arch rivals of Rangers Football Club or *Andra's Heroes* as he called them – favourites of the city's Protestant population. There was great rivalry between the two clubs and their supporters. Andra almost burst a blood vessel when he stood out on that verandah for the first time and saw that green patch of Celtic's grass. He was sure this was a ploy of Glasgow's city fathers to get at him.

Andra was one of the blinkered minority that plagued both camps. He was a super bigot *and* a racist. The Rangers supporters had booted him out of their club because of his over-the-top bigoted behaviour. The distinguished Orange Lodge had also ostracised him for bringing their order into disrepute and his efforts to join the Freemasons had all of his applications despatched to the wastepaper bin.

Life for Andra was at a low ebb. Not only to be incarcerated in this high up purgatory with the view of Celtic Park forever within eyeshot, his wife being a devout Catholic, his daughter, Jean, marrying a Jew and his only son, Peter in a seminary studying for the priesthood, it was now up to himself to redeem his life . . . he had already moved in that direction.

Jean took up the feather duster and went round the room flicking and cleaning. She straightened the frame of the magnificent painting of King Billy astride his horse, that had Andra's pride of place on the wall above the sideboard – adjacent to the picture of himself in his Rangers regalia taken in happier times. In the same frame although facing the wall was a picture of Pope Pius the tenth, put there by Annie "jist tae even things up".

On top of the sideboard was a nine-inch plaster statue of Saint Francis of Assisi, a gift from Peter to his mother on one of his visits. Andra likened and referred to it, as "one of the dwarves". In reply, Annie had her own name for King William of Orange.

The bickering never ceased but, deep down, the pair had a great affection for each other though they seldom showed it.

Jean, now quite satisfied with her work, flopped on to the moquette settee. She closed her eyes and was startled by the loud shrill of the telephone.

"Who?" Jean inquired. "Oh, yes . . . hello Mr Maxwell," she went on, recognising the voice. "Nope, Mum and Dad haven't arrived home from their holiday yet – yes, I'm just waiting – they should be arriving any time now – oh, definitely they will be wanting their morning milk as usual. Where – oh, they were in the Eternal City – no, not Ibrox – ROME – yes, I'll tell them you called – yes a pint – and make sure it's the blue top milk and not the green top – yes, Dad nearly had a heart attack when he saw it – and *orange* juice please. That Limeade you left the last time made him go berserk – you know what he's like – thanks for calling." She hung up.

⋆   ⋆   ⋆

The plane from Rome began its descent over the Campsie Hills *en route* to Glasgow Airport. Andra Thomson edged closer to the window, which he rubbed vigorously with his cuff, and took a deep breath. "Ah, God's ain country!" he sighed.

Annie, his long suffering wife, sighed too.In a way she was glad that their Roman holiday was over. Annie was tired of listening to his moans and groan since the day they landed at Rome's Leonardio da Vinci Airport two weeks earlier. Annie was surprised that Andra had agreed to accompany her to the Eternal City in the first place. Rome was never mentioned when Wee Hughie Broon purchased the ticket as a gift for Andra. Her husband almost had a cardiac arrest when he heard that his prize was a trip for two to Rome.

The plane landed smoothly.

"Nae bother!" Andra said, turning to Annie.

The smartly-dressed stewardess, standing by the door, nodded to Andra and Annie as they squeezed past.

"Ma compliments tae the driver, "Andra said, acknowledging her greeting. "Ah couldnae have done better masel'."

Annie nudged her husband in the ribs and shoved him through the door. They gingerly made their way down the steps to the tarmac where Andra pulled himself up to his full height and filled his lungs with the chilled air of the morning.

"Aye!" he exclaimed. "We are back hame in God's ain country. Ah can smell the pitch frae here."

"We don't have pitch here," Annie said. "That's the tarmac ye smell."

"Ah'm talkin' aboot the glorious Ibrox pitch," Andra snapped.
Annie shook her head in despair and led the way to the baggage-claim carousel.

Collecting their luggage, they headed towards the Customs entrances.

Andra stopped suddenly, his eyes scanning the excise unit.

"C'mon you," Annie snapped as she saw a sharp-eyed customs' officer eyeing Andra and knitting his brows.

"We've got nothin' tae declare," Annie said, "so we go through this way," nodding towards the green exit.

"Ah am not passin' under that sign," Andra said angrily. "No way!"

Annie put down her heavy case and, hands on hips, snapped, "Right, then, whit colour suits ye, eh? Are ye goin' through the *red* gate?"

"Ah don't see how no' – seein' ah was nearly a member o' the Brigton Croass Communist Party," Andra said proudly.

"In yer dreams, son," Annie retorted and, lugging her suitcase, marched through to the green zone.

Andra, pulling his wheeled case, turned sharply and walked through the red zone. There was no way he was going to walk under the green hue.

He was immediately stopped by a stern-faced, middle-aged customs officer. "Read this, sir," he said to Andra, handing him a clip board.

"Ah have forgot to bring ma readin' glesses," Andra said.

"Have you anything to declare?" the man asked

"Ah have just declared that ah forgot for tae bring ma readin' glesses," Andra replied irritably.

"Have you any tobacco or alcohol you wish to declare?"

"*Alcohol!*" Andra almost screamed. "Never mention that dreaded word tae me. It is the ruin o' ma life. Every time Ah look at ma dear wife Annie . . ." Andra shook his head sadly. "Two bottles o'vodka a day . . . plastered every minute she is." Andra dabbed his eyes. "Noo, can ye no' see why Ah hate that word. *Hate* it!" he emphasised. "Just lookin' at a boattle drives her intae a frenzy."

The customs man was having none of it. "Are you saying that you are not carrying any alcohol?"

"Think Ah'm daft?" Andra said with a look of innocence. "Ah've got the only wife in Glesca that lies oan the flair tae dae the ironin'. Oor dug's an alcoholic just by sniffin' her breath. Ah've got tae add a gill o' whisky intae his *Bounce* before he'll go near it. It's sad tae see that wee dug staggerin' doon the street stoappin' at every lamp post. Ma poor wife, Annie, Ah can see her there hingin' oot the windae, drunk as a puggy. It's a horrible sight." Andra shook his head once more.

"Most Glesca wimmen hang oot the windae," the officer said.

"No' by their apron strings tied tae the sink,they don't," Andra said.

The customs officer frowned. He was not going to believe this cock-and-bull story. "Right," he snapped. "Open your case."

Reluctantly, Andra opened up.

The officer rummaged through the contents. With a cry of triumph, he pulled out six bottles of *Bells* whisky. "Ah-Ha!" he exclaimed. "Whit's this?"

"It's no' for me," Andra said.

"Ah suppose it's for the wife, eh?" the man said sceptically.

"Naw, she only drinks vodka," Andra said.

"It's for the dug, then?"

"Naw, he's a Irish Terrier, only drinks *Bushmills*."

"Right then," the officer snapped. "Ye either pey duty or Ah'll have tae confiscate these."

Andra's jaw dropped. "How can *you* charge me duty for these when a' Ah was daein' was helpin' ma – *oor* – country's exports? This isnae Tequila or vodka Ah am bringin' in. It's ma – *oor* – ain country's produce. You should look on me as a patriot, so ye should. Ah should nut be staunin' here sufferin' like this. Ah had enough sufferin' in that infernal city Ah've jist left – where Ah purchased this medicinal spirit."

The customs man narrowed his eyes. "Ah don't care if ye bought it in Timbuktu. Ye'll have tae pay up."

Andra stuck his fingers in his ears. "Ye can make me pey for ma medicine but Ah do nut have for tae get insulted."

"Ah didnae insult ye," the man protested."Whit did Ah say?"

"Ye said the wan word that sticks in ma throat," Andra snapped back. "That word ma delicate ears will nut tolerate – *Tim*."

"Ah never said nae such thing," the man complained.

"Ye did so, " Andra said. "Ye said *Tim*bucktoo."

The customs man was getting fed up with this clown. "Right," he said. "Are you peyin' duty or no'?"

"Ah pey ma duty tae king an' country every twelfth," Andra said, sticking out his chest.

"Very well, sir,"the official said, "I'll give you a receipt for this contraband."

Andra, dejected, left the customs hall minus his precious carry-out. He cursed the customs man saying he should have been more patriotic.

Annie was already through and standing impatiently by the open door of a taxi – drumming her fingers on its roof.

"Whit kept you?" she snapped.

"A traitor in there," he said. Jabbing his thumb towards the exit door.

Annie threw a despairing glance towards heaven and they climbed into the cab. "London Road, driver," Annie said. "Just past Celtic Park," she added with satisfaction. She ignored her husband's groan.

She knew when she married Andra that he was a true and committed "bluenose" – a staunch Protestant – while she was committed to her faith – a stanch Catholic – a dreadful secret that Andra had fought to keep from his pals. It would never do for Andra Thomson, proud of his voice that rose above all others at Ibrox Park, Rangers' hallowed ground, to be married to a Catholic. Only Hughie Broon knew and he was bound to secrecy. Andra was, in a sense, although he would never admit it, proud of his wee pal. Never once had Hughie let it slip that Andra's daughter, Jean, had married a Jewish chap or, God forbid, that his son, Peter, was studying for the Catholic priesthood. Yes. Hughie had never let him down.

Jean's husband Clarence was, to Andra's way of thinking, at least a Jew – neutral. But Peter, again, to Andra's way of think-ing, had been brainwashed by Annie and was temporarily insane.

Andra wondered why God was making him suffer so. He had never done anything to anger him – except that time when he banged the big drum harder as they passed Sacred Heart Chapel in Old Dalmarnock road. That was in happier days before he was thrown out o' the *ludge*. Even his precious booze being confiscated at the airport was *His* work, he was sure. Hadn't *He* stuck the knife in when *He* answered Annie's prayers and moved them into this high hell-hole – up on the twenty-seventh floor. Maybe, Andra thought, *He* wanted Annie a wee bit nearer. But to be overlooking Celtic Park? That was really turning he screw.

Andra had to be rushed to the Royal Infirmary the day they first entered their new high-rise flat. He had stepped on to the balcony and immediately he spotted what was down below – Celtic Park – he wanted to throw himself over. Instead, he just collapsed. Annie was in seventh heaven. A new home with a *bath* and a *toilet*. Everything she had prayed for. She made a novena in thanksgiving. All she wanted now to make her life complete was to see Peter ordained. She had thanked God that Jean was happily married. Jean had picked a good, hard working man, and now lived in Utopia – known as Newton Mearns.

Clarence's dad was a doctor. He and his wife's visits to the Thomsons were now few and far between. Andra had put that down to the fact that they had moved into the high flat and that Clarence's mother was afraid of heights.

Annie knew better. She knew it was because every time her daughter's in-laws paid a visit the good doctor made to examine Andra's 'bad back'. The doctor had decided that Andra's bad back was as strong as an ox and probably putting some hard work into it would help.

The taxi drew up at the Thomson's skyscraper block. Andra was delighted that the driver had heard his request and had "put the foot down" passing Celtic Park. Although the park was a blur as they speeded by, Andra had still time to stick out his tongue accompanied by the loudest raspberry he could manage.

Jean wiped her brow as they alighted. She hoped the lift would be working. The driver hauled the heavy cases from the boot – the ones with the ribbons tied to their handles for easy recognition as they came round the baggage-claim carousel – the blue and white ribbons. Andra glided through the close pulling his wheeled case as Annie struggled in his wake, panting and hauling her heavy belongings. She was delighted that the lift was still working and was waiting for them.

Andra fumbled for his keys. He had pressed the doorbell not expecting it to be answered but just to hear the melodious tones of *The Sash* echoing from inside.

Jean opened the door before he could find his keys. Jean threw her arms around her parents' necks. Kissing Annie on the cheek, she flustered, "Oh, mum," happy to see them home safely.

Andra had walked straight in and, immediately, his eyes were drawn to the figure of St Francis. Pointing shaking fingers, he blurted. "Whit's Ronnie Corbett daein there?"

"Noo Andra," Annie said, "we've had a' this oot before, remember? Ah could keep ma Ron – er – St Francis statue and you could keep yer life-sized inflatable Derek Johnstone." Derek Johnstone being one of the Rangers football team star players.

Andra grunted. He had made this deal in a blind moment after Annie had chucked his Derek Johnstone over the balcony.

"I'll make a cup of tea," Jean said, vanishing into the kitchen.

"Aw. That would be lovely, hen," Annie said.

"No' for me," Andra called. Going over to the sideboard and pushing St Francis aside he retrieved a bottle of Johnny Walker. Andra filled a glass and, standing erect before the picture of King Billy, raised his glass. "Your Majesty," he said with awe, "Ah'm hame."

He was sure that His Majesty had missed him the last fortnight. He only hoped his royal personage did not know where he had been. Andra knocked back the drink in a single gulp. "Ah," he sighed smacking his lips, "a real drink at last. Ah've been drinkin' Mr Sheen for the last fortnight. They call it vino, Ah call it pee-o – good for poalishin' furniture right enough."

"Ach, away ye go," Annie said, "Ye managed tae get a few boattles ower yer trap anyway."

"Ah had for tae have somethin' tae swally ma blood pressure pills ower wi'," Andra grunted.

"It's aboot time ye swallied yer daft pride," Annie said.

Jean entered with the tea and joined her mother at the table.

They sipped and Anne sighed. "Aw, nice tae get a wee cuppa tea again!" she exclaimed with satisfaction.

"So," Jean said, "how did you two like Rome?"

Annie clasped her hands to her breast and looked towards

heaven. "Oh, Jean, it was wonderful. We saw the Pope on his balcony," she said, all a flutter.

Andra sneered.

"He came oot oan his balcony a' in his white robes and waved tae everybody."

"Ah thought he was the windae cleaner," Andra said sarcastically.

Annie knew that Andra was winding her up. He knew fine it was the Pope up there blessing them. She caught him often enough with his two fingers in the air and his tongue sticking out – not to mention the foul noises coming from his mouth.

"I take it that you did not enjoy your Roman holiday, Dad?" Jean said, pecking his cheek affectionately.

"Full o' bloody foreigners," Andra snarled. "Spaghetti – spaghetti – spaghetti – that's a' they eat."

"Bolognaise?" Jean said.

"Aye, that's whit Ah say," Andra replied.

"Were you not taken by the splendour of the place?" Jean asked. "The awe – the art – the beautiful buildings? Saint Peter's Square?"

"Aye, well, that's his business," Andra said. "His personality's got nothin' tae dae wi' me. The place is full o' penguins a' waddlin' aboot. Italy's supposed for tae be the land o' style. Italian claeths an' a' that – the envy o' the world. That's a laugh. Ye should see the gear some o' they blokes wore – straight oot o' Ali Baba – ridiculous, so it is."

"Ye didnae have tae go and ask them for two tickets for the matinee and gie me a red face, did ye?" Annie snapped.

"Ach, Ah thought that's whit they were daein' – sellin' tickets," Andra said.

"They were Swiss Guards," Annie said angrily, "the Pope's bodyguard frae hunners o' years ago, it's tradition. And they penguins are *nuns*, ya ignorant get."

"If they ur the Pope's bodyguards frae hunners o' years ago," Andra retorted, "how come their uniforms were designed by Walt Disney?"

"Their uniforms were designed by the great artist Michaelangelo," Jean put in.

"Him that played for that great Italian team, Real Madrid?"

Andra asked, proud of his knowledge of European football.

"He didnae play for Rangers, that's for sure, "Annie said facetiously.

"Michaelangelo was a great sculptor and artist, Dad," Jean said. "He painted the Sistine Chapel."

"If he's got anythin' tae dae wi' the chapel, how would Ah know him?" Andra snapped.

"He was one of the world's greatest artists," Jean went on. "His full name was Michaelangelo Buonarroti."

"A Welshman, eh!" Andra remarked seriously, wondering how a Welshman had anything to do with Roman art.

"It took him four years to paint the Sistine Chapel," Jean volunteered.

"It took yer faither four years tae paint oor stairheid lavvy in the auld buildin'," Annie said.

"That was because auld Wullie McLatchie was never oot it," Andra complained. "Ah used tae staun on the stairheid waitin' for him tae come oot. Then Ah'd hear a flush, he would step oot – then turn aboot and go right back in again. That auld swine was definitely incont . . . er . . . incon . . . er incognito!"

"So, you definitely did not enjoy your holiday, Dad?" Jean said, but with a knowing smile.

"Ah'll tell ye this," Andra said, clenching his fists, "Ah'll murder Wee Hughie when Ah get ma hauns on him." Then, mimicking his wee pal, he went on, "Ah bought ye this raffle ticket, Andra, frae a wee wumman ootside McDougall's." Steam blew from Andra's ears. "Ah'll kill the wee swine, so Ah will."

"Ye canny blame wee Hughie," Annie said, coming to the diminutive man's defence. "He bought you that ticket in good faith. He thought he was daein' you a good turn – a wee kindness."

Andra snorted. "Imagine winnin' a prize for a hoaliday in hell – a trip tae the infernal city," Andra grimaced. "*Me!* Could it no' have been an adventure hoaliday somewhere – fishin' or somethin'? Ah like fishin' – sittin' there oan ma wee stool, ma rod in ma haun – jist watchin' the wee fishes swimmin' doon the river – the Boyne, of coorse. Noo, widnae that have been somethin. Eh? Just me, the wee fishes an' the flowin' Boyne?" Andra clicked his tongue, "Aye, that would've been something!

Anyway," he went on, "Ah'll get the wee nyaff in ma ain time. Right noo a' Ah want tae hear is whit was the score at the old Firm gemme oan Setturday, Jean?"

"Twelve nothing, Dad," Jean said with nonchalance.

"Aw, ya beauty!!"Andra cried, throwing his arms into the air.

"For Celtic, dad," his daughter added quietly.

A sudden silence descended. Andra's jaw fell open. He clutched his chest – on the right side – and collapsed on to the couch.

"Ah'm sufferin' – sufferin'," he moaned. "It's ma punishment for strayin' away tae Penguin County." His groans grew louder.

Annie patted her husband's cheek and, with a wry smile, said, "Wan for each apostle, Andra, eh?"

"Ah wondered why that crowd went intae a frenzy when the Pope came oot tae the balcony, cupped his hauns and shouted, '*Twelve-a nuthin*'. Ah didnae know whit he was talkin' aboot."

"He said nae such thing," Annie snapped. "He was talkin' Italian."

"Well, it sounded like twelve nothin' tae me," Andra said dismally.

"Never mind, Dad," Jean said, pecking his cheek, "there'll be other times. Tell me, what was the entertainment like?"

"Rubbish!!" Andra cried. "The place is full o' beggars. Ye couldnae walk doon the street without hivin' a haun shoved under yer nose. Even wee weans were at it. They were sittin' in doorways their wee hauns stretched oot, lire – lire – they were sayin."

"You should've felt sorry for them, "Annie said. "Ye didnae have tae say 'Wan, two, three a-lire,' back ."

"You find kids in every every European country begging, Dad," Jean said.

"No' still in their nappies, wi' their dummies in their mooths," Andra said.

"Oh, you're exaggerating," Jean said.

"Am Ah!" Andra retorted. "Wan wean was still sittin' oan his potty."

Jean turned quizzically to her mother who threw a glance at the ceiling.

"So, things couldn't have been that bad," Jean went on. "What about the night life?"

"Nane," Andra said with contempt. "Somebody suggested we go tae the Colosseum. See when we got there?" Andra's voice became more bitter. "It was a con. There was nae pictures showin'. Ah thought the Geggie was bad but that Colosseum was fa'in' tae bits. No' only did it have nae seats, it had nae bloody roof. Call that a picture hall?" He screwed up his nose.

"Not a cinema, Dad," Jean corrected. "That's where the gladiators of their day met for the great fights."

Andra was suddenly interested. "Oh, the Rangers an' Celtic o' their day, eh?"

"Nero used to sit and watch the lions fight and eat the Christians," Jean explained.

"How did the lions know which wans were the Catholics?" Andra asked, bringing down his brows.

"There were no Catholics then," Jean said.

Andra's eyes lit up. "Imagine," he said, "a land wi' nae papes. Don't tell me they lions just ate proddies?" he grimaced.

"There were no Protestants and no Catholics then," Jean said, "Just Christians."

"Ach, that widnae work noo-a-days," Andra shrugged. "Big drum and flute makers would go oot o' business. Fishmongers would have tae shut on a Friday for that other crowd. Naw, it widnae work. Too many people made idle."

CHAPTER TWO

WEE HUGHIE BROON LEFT MCDOUGALL'S WITH HALF A BOTTLE of Bells whisky and six cans of lager in a brown paper bag. Andra, his big china, would have arrived home by now from his super holiday and would, no doubt, be eager to thank him for making it all possible.

He was pleased the lift was already in the closemouth waiting for him. Hughie stepped in and pressed the button for the twenty-seventh floor. He staggered slightly as the lift burst into life and began its ascent. Aye, Andra would be pleased to see him – *and* his brown paper bag.

Hughie stepped out of the lift, got his bearings and weaved his way to the Thomsons' bright blue and white painted door. He pressed the doorbell and, clutching his parcel to his chest, did a jig as the melodious sound of *The Sash* echoed from inside.

Andra had problems with Annie when he decided to introduce this mode of alerting that someone was at the door. He wanted the entire block to know where his loyalties lay and it took Annie all her arguing and threatening to stop him from attaching a microphone to the doorbell connected to a loudspeaker on the outside of the building. They finally compromised. Andra could have his musical doorbell – but *no* loudspeaker – with its burst of *The Sash* – *if* alternately the tune changed to the dulcet tones of *Immaculate Mary*.

Andra, too, did a jig when the doorbell rang.

"I'll get it," Jean said, and vanished into the lobby. "It's Hughie," she said, announcing Andra's diminutive pal and ushering him into the living room.

Hughie, a water-melon smile on his face, did not know what he was walking into.

Andra leapt from his chair, and darted across the room grabbing a surprised Hughie around the neck and began to throttle him. "Ya wee swine," he hollered. "A raffle ticket tae hell – that's whit ye gave me."

Hughie choked. "Ah . . . ah . . ." he gasped.

Annie jumped up and got herself in between them. Prising them apart, she bawled. "Stoap it – stoap it Andra – look, he's turnin' blue!"

"Right colour!" Andra snapped.

Hughie gulped in air as Andra's grip loosened

"Ya wee nyaff," Andra said through gritted teeth.

"Ah – Ah – didnae know it was a foartnight in Ro . . . Ro . . . *that* place," Hughie gasped.

"Hughie thought he was daein' you a favour when he bought that raffle ticket, don't you forget that," Annie said, in the wee man's defence.

"That's right, Andra," Hughie pleaded. "Ah'm yer freen."

"You ur a poison dwarf," Andra said. "A freen widnae let me go through that torture, so he widnae."

"Ah thought it was a wee wumman sellin' tickets," Hughie said.

"Aye, well just you watch who ye buy yer raffles frae," Andra said, calming down. "Did the horns stickin' oot her heid no' make ye suspicious?"

"Whit horns?" Hughie asked, knitting his brows.

"She was a *nun*, wint she?" Andra sniped. "So she must've had horns."

"Away ye go ya glaiket moron," Annie said angrily. "Ah could say that the Rangers should have forked tails and cloven hooves."

"You wash yer mooth oot," Andra retorted. "If they had cloven hooves they couldnae score a' they wonderful goals that they score." Andra was not amused at his wife's 'forked' tongue.

"Oh, aye, *twelve-nothin'*,eh?" Annie licked her finger and marked up a score in the air

"We a' hiv oor off days," Andra said sulkily.

"You have them every day," Annie said.

Getting fed up with this bickering but grateful to Annie for saving his life, Hughie brought out his half bottle of Bells and his six cans of lager.

"A wee dram, Andra," he said holding up the whisky, "for tae celebrate youse comin' hame safely."

Andra's eyes lit up and, getting a couple of glasses from the sideboard, he wasted no time in filling them – half-inch for

Hughie, two inches for himself.

"Ah'll let you aff this time but in future just watch it, Hughie or you'll become hauf-a-pun o' mince. Only buy yer raffle tickets frae somebody ye know – somebody wearin' a blue an' white scarf and wi' a beard comin' doon tae his chest."

"Like Santy Claus?" Hughie's eyebrows raised.

"Like somebody that resembles John Knox," Andra said.

"Whit if it's a wumman that's sellin' the raffles?" Hughie asked quizzically?"

"Well, in that case, Mrs John Knox." Andra replied, casting his eyes up in despair.

"How am Ah tae know whit Missus Knox looks like?" Hughie asked, worriedly.

"Right enough," Andra said. "You probably don't even know whit yer ain maw looks like."

"Ah hivnae seen ma maw for a while, right enough," Hughie said sadly.

"Aw, whit a shame!" Annie said. "When *did* ye last see yer mammy, Hughie?"

"When Ah was six month auld," Hughie said, puckering his lip.

"How was that?" Jean asked.

"She gave me away," Hughie said.

"Wi' a coupon like yours Ah canny blame 'er," Andra said sarcastically.

"You shut up," Annie snapped.

"You mean she put you up for adoption?" Jean said.

"Naw, Ah was just lyin' there in ma wee pram when she picked me up an' haunded me tae a wee wumman that was just passin'."

"Whit did she dae that for?" Annie said in disbelief.

"Ah don't know," Hughie shrugged. "Ah heard her stoapppin that wee wumman an' askin' her if she liked ugly weans and when she said she did she gave her me."

"Whit a terrible thing to do," Jean shook her head.

"Jist whit Ah said," Andra said. "Ah mean wan night we were walkin' doon the road when a full moon came oot and he turned a' hairy. Frightenin' it was. Wan minute Ah was walkin' doon the street wi' Hughie and the next Ah was walkin' wi' Yogi Bear."

"It's a gene that runs in the family," Hughie said, his head bowed.

"His faither won first prize at Crufts wance, "Andra added.

"Ah had tae stoap goin' tae Barraland," Hughie said.

"How was that?" Jean asked. "Was it in case it happened when you were walking a girl home?"

"Naw, no' really," Hughie said. "Every time Billy McGregor and the Gaybirds struck up *Moonlight Serenade* Ah had tae run like hell."

"Ah don't believe any o' this tripe," Annie snapped. "Ah know yer faither – a nice wee man wi' a' long, black beard."

"That's his maw," Andra said.

"Right, enough o' this. Hughie, we had a wonderful holiday thanks tae you."

"Good!" Hughie said. "And, Andra – did ye see the p . . . pp . . . ppp — *him*, – did ye?"

"The word is *Pope*, Hughie," Annie said. "And it's no' a bad word."

"He came oot oan a wee ledge, Hughie . . . and he spotted me right away," Andra grimaced. "It was humiliatin'."

"How dae ye know he spotted ye?" Hughie asked, in disbelief.

"He waved tae me, Hughie and oor eyes met," Andra said. "Ah shouted up tae him in ma loudest Ibrox voice: 'Dae ye want a season ticket for Ibrox?'"

"Whit did he say?" Hughie asked, shocked that Andra had even opened his mouth and deigned to converse with *Him*.

"He shouted 'Alleluia, Alleluia . . . ya beauty'."

"Ally who?" Hughie asked.

"It's no' Ally anybody ya wee idiot," Andra said, tutting. "It's . . . er . . . it's er . . . wan o' them Catholic words in their language . . . Satin."

"*Latin*, ya *big* idiot," Annie said, "And it's nothin' tae dae wi' 'them Catholic words'. His Holiness probably never heard ye."

"Well, thank God he didnae say 'Aye', that he would love a season ticket for Ibrox," Hughie said. "Ah don't think it would've went doon wi the boys in McDougall's . . . besides there's no' spare seat oan the bus, so there's no'."

"Youse are talkin' absolute rubbish," Annie said. "He was cryin' oot a shout of praise, that's a', nothin' tae dae wi' Ibrox."

"It *was* so," Andra protested. "If Ah had come hame wi' the p . . . p . . ." Andra took a deep breath, "Pope as a Rangers supporter they would have made me chairman o' the supporters' club."

"*Chairman!?*" Annie cried. "You're no' even a member yersel', remember? *You* were chucked oot because o' yer bigoted attitude. Annie put in the final twist of the screw. "Naebody wants tae know ye, Andra – the Ludge, the masons – naebody."

Andra was hurt. But he would never show it. "Naebody?" he whispered.

"No' even the Brigton Croass Communist Party," Annie said, suddenly feeling sorry for her husband. "Ah'm talkin' aboot official bodies, ye understaun'," she added quickly.

Andra brightened. "Ach, Ah'm still no' with it," he said. "Ah've got jet lag and the thought o' they two weeks in hell have drained me."

"It's usually you that's daein' the drainin', eh, Andra?" Hughie said.

"You shut yer face," Andra snapped.

"*Jet lag?*" Annie yelled. "Andra it takes you longer tae get intae toon oan the caur, so it does. And don't you dare call beautiful Rome hell. You should be gled that Hughie gave ye the chance tae go tae that wonderful city."

"Hughie," Andra said, "the whole place is a sham. Take the Colosseum for instance, nae seats, nae roof—"

Hughie suddenly got brave. He held up his hand. "Naw, naw, Andra," he said, pulling himself up to his full height. "Credit where it's due. Their Colosseum is no' like oor Colosseum in Eglinton Street." He suddenly pulled down his arm in case it got broken. "Ah saw Charleton Heston in that great Septic, *Ben Casey,* and it a' took place in the Colosseum. There was this chari – chari – charcoal race roon it. And everybody cheered. Great picture so it was."

"Ach, Colosseum or no'," Annie butted in, "it was a great hoaliday. Ye gave Andra some education, Hughie. Just think, Andra, ye can always say ye visited the land o' the great Michaelangelo, the painter."

"They say he invented Dulux," Hughie said innocently.

"It was also the land o' the great Leonardo – a marvellous artist," Annie said, adding, "he painted the Mona Lisa and was a great inventor as well."

23

"Oh, and whit did *he* invent?" Andra said, not wanting to praise any of Annie's Italian heroes.

"The helicopter," Annie said, proud to show off her knowledge of Roman history. "He was a man before his time."

"He wisnae the only man who invented things before his time," Andra said.

"Who are ye talkin' aboot?" Annie asked with some scepticism.

"His Majesty up there, who else," Andra said, jabbing his thumb at the wall painting.

"Who? Oor Wullie," Annie laughed.

"Ah have warned ye *never* tae address Oor...er...His Majesty as Oor Wullie!" Andra cried.

"And whit did he invent?" Annie said, her brows descending.

"You tell her, Hughie," Andra said, turning to his pal.

Hughie thought for a moment. "Er . . . er . . . *The Walk?*" he said at last.

"Exactly," Andra said, patting him on the back.

"Ye canny call that an invention," Annie laughed. "Folk have been walkin' for years before Oor Wullie came alang."

"So you say," Andra said. "We walk majestically noo – oor heids held high. Us homosap . . . er . . . homosap . . ."

"Homosexuals," Hughie volunteered. "Ah read that wance."

"Aye, them, we used for tae walk on all fours," Andra agreed.

"You still dae that on a Saturday," Annie said.

Hughie thought he would change the subject. "How did ye like flyin', Andra?" he asked.

"That's the condition he's in as well on a Saturday," Annie said.

"Rotten," Andra said, screwing up his nose. "It was stiflin' oan that plane and naebody would open a windae."

"Ye're no' supposed tae open windaes, Andra," Hughie said. "Look whit happened tae the ex-president o' oor supporters' club, wee Erchie Smith."

"Whit happened tae him?" Annie asked curiously.

"Erchie was runnin' away wi' a wee Catholic barmaid and he decided tae open the windae on the plane when naebody would listen tae him."

"Where was he goin'?" Annie asked.

"County Cork where his wee lover lived," Hughie said. "His wife wisnae pleased so she wisnae."

'Cos he was runnin' away wi' his fancy wumman?" Annie went on.

"Naw, because she was a *Catholic* barmaid," Hughie said angrily.

"Ye mean it would've been a'right if it had been a Proddy barmaid?" Annie said.

"Ah'm a bit surprised masel – anyway, Erchie was sittin' there sweatin' and finally took things intae his ain hauns." Hughie said.

"Whit did he dae?" Annie shuffled to the edge of her chair.

"He took oot a spanner he happened for tae have in his poacket and smashed the windae. He wisnae caring aboot a heavy fine."

"An' did he get a heavy fine?"Annie asked.

"Ah don't know," Hughie said. "We never saw him again."

"Serves him right!" Annie said, tightening her lip. "He should never have been runnin' away at a'."

"Or vanished wi' a good Proddy barmaid," Andra added.

"He deserves a' he gets," Annie said, "him a married man."

"Ah always had ma doots aboot Wee Erchie,"Andra said. "Ah mean he used for tae turn up at the bus his face a' painted."

"Och, Andra," Hughie said, "a loat of the boys turn up for the gemme wi' their faces painted."

"No' wi' powder an' red lipstick and that massacre stuff, they don't," Andra said.

"So, you think he shouldnae have run away wi' a barmaid, Andra, eh? Is it because she was Irish?" Annie asked.

"That as well, "Andra replied.

"As well as whit?" Annie said.

"Ah was surprised Erchie had run away wi' a barmaid – a bar*man*, aye, but no' a barmaid," Andra said.

"Me tae, "Hughie agreed. "Ye'know, Andra, Ah really got a big surprise wan day when Ah was staunin' next tae wee Erchie outside the bus. Ah had nae idea he was – er – funny till Ah happened for tae mention that Ah was dyin' for a smoke."

"And?" Andra's brows went up.

"Well Erchie went intae his handbag and gied me a fag,"

Hughie said with a smug expression, adding, "Ah was really shocked, so Ah was."

"Because o' his handbag?" Andra asked.

"Naw, Ah didnae know he smoked," Hughie said.

"Was he gay?" Annie asked.

"Well, he did laugh a loat, right enough." Andra said.

Jean decided to change the subject. "You won't have heard that your next door neighbours have left?" she said.

"Aw, no' the O'Reillys?" Annie said, her hand coming up to her mouth.

"I'm afraid so," Jean said.

"Did they take their ten weans wi' them?" Andra asked, obvious joy in his voice.

"Of course," Jean said.

"Thank God for that," Andra said with relief. "Hughie," he said, turning to his pal, "Ah'm sure they wurnae weans at a'. A' ye heard a' day was chantin', chantin', chantin'. Ah'm positive they were a' midget priests."

"Don't be stupit," Annie sniped. "Midget priests!" she said with contempt. "Ah've never heard anythin' so ridiculous in ma life – except maybe for that time when you said you'd got a joab."

"Hughie, ye should've seen their washin' line – nothin' but a row o' dog collars," Andra argued.

"They *were* the dug's collars," Annie insisted.

"Ye mean the dug was a priest?" Hughie said, shaking his head.

"You're as daft as him," Annie said, nodding towards Andra.

"Between the O'Reillys and that Randy wan, it was like livin' in a monastery," Andra grimaced.

"Who is Randy?" Hughie asked.

"Another chanter, Hughie," Andra moaned. "A' night ye could no' only hear him, ye could smell 'im – walkin' up an' doon chantin' wi' wan o' they incest sticks in his haun, wearin' nuthin' but a big orange sheet."

"Well, he has the colour right," Hughie said.

"That's aboot a'," Andra said.

"Did he no' have a blanket?" asked Hughie.

"Naw, jist that orange sheet wrapped roon' 'im," Andra said. "He is a follower o' Harry Lauder."

"Hare Krishna," Annie corrected.

"Aye, him as well, " Andra said.

"Yes, well it's not *is*, Dad, it's *was* . . . Randy got killed," Jean said sadly.

"Oh naw, Annie said, shocked. "Whit happened, Jean?"

"He was shooing a pigeon away from his balcony and toppled over," Jean said.

"Whit happened tae the doo?" Andra asked.

"Never mind the pigeon," Annie snapped, scowling at Andra. "Poor Randy, such a nice boy!"

"Two birds wi' wan stone!" Andra showed his delight. "The O'Reillys and Randy Pandy. Boy, is God good tae me!" He sighed deeply.

"Did the O'Reillys leave tae go back tae Ireland, Jean?" Annie asked.

"No," Jean shook her head. "They were scared away. They said the house was haunted."

Andra burst out laughing. "*Haunted?*" he guffawed. "Whit a load o' tripe! Ah'm tellin' ye, the only spirits in that hoose came oot o'a boattle o' Bushmills. *Haunted?* Ha!!"

"Maybe it is that Randy wan," Hughie volunteered, "still lookin' for that pigeon."

"Ah don't think so, Hughie," Andra said. "Ye don't come back frae the hereafter tae go pigeon huntin'."

"Poor Randolph!" was all Annie could say.

"His fa' might've been safter if he'd been wearin' a blanket," Hughie said seriously.

"We are up twenty-seven flairs, Hughie," Andra reminded him. "He'd have needed for tae be wearin' a parachute."

"So, ye could say it was a 'blue doo' for him, eh?" Hughie quipped.

Andra laughed loudly.

"Yes, well, I'll have to run!" Jean said heading for the door. "Clarence will be coming home soon from work and will be looking for his supper."

"Clarence!" Andra said with disgust, throwing his eyes towards the ceiling. "Whit will ye be gien' him? Camel meat?"

Annie scowled.

"He'll be getting his favorite – haggis and neeps and mashed potato," Jean said, annoyed at her father's bigotry.

"Huh!" Andra grunted as Jean left.

Jean was used to her father's attitude to her husband. Anybody or anything that did not fit into Andra's world was alien. She had watched her mother try to prise the blinkers from her dad for years but saw it was a hopeless case. She sympathised with Annie, strong in her faith and hurt terribly at her husband's attitude towards their son Peter. Andra had to be rushed to the Glasgow Eye Infirmary one day when he walked in and saw Peter in the room dressed in the brown Franciscan habit Annie had purchased for him.

"Jist tae see how ye'll look son efter you're ordained," she said proudly.

Andra had complained that his retina had been dislodged.

* * *

The door opened and Jean, sorry that she hadn't said a proper goodbye, returned. She pecked her mother on the cheek, hesitated and kissed her father.

"It's lovely to have you both home safely," she said and, with a cheeky smile, added, "And I'm glad you enjoyed yourself, Dad." With a grin, she closed the door behind her.

Andra puffed his chest out. "Aye, right enough," he said, "it *is* great for tae be hame in God's ain country – among freens and auld familiar faces." To emphasise his delight he stood before his pictured hero, snapped heels and saluted smartly.

Annie threw a glance at the ceiling. "Aye, we're hame right enough," she murmured. "Och, Ah we'll miss . . . Mrs O'Reilly," she sighed.

"No' me," Andra said, "You just miss her for getting' her doon tae chapel an' that. Ah hope they a' went back tae Ireland. Scots for the Scots, that's whit Ah say. There's nae room for foreigners here. We are a wee country and hivnae got room for them and maist o' them claimin' benefit an a' – aye, Scots for the Scots, that's whit Ah say." Andra had a smug expression.

"Me tae," said Hughie.

"Whit aboot Oor Wullie there," Annie said, nodding towards the picture.

"Ah've telt ye *never*, but *never*, refer tae Oor – er – His Majesty as oor – you know. Anywey, whit aboot him?"

"He's Dutch or somethin'," Annie said smugly.

"Ahhh!" Andra said with a grin. "He spoke wi' a Scoatch accent."

"Ah read he had bad teeth," Annie said.

"Better than your maw auld Gumsy Gladys."

" Ah know whit it's like for tae hiv nae teeth," Hughie piped up.

"Is that false teeth ye hiv, Hughie?" Annie asked.

"Naw. These are ma ain," the wee man replied.

"How can ye have nae teeth and suddenly ye hiv?" Andra grumbled.

"Ah was only two months auld when Ah was gumsy," Hughie said, hurt.

"Ach away ye go ya daft wee idiot," Andra said. "Anywey, your infantile gub has nothin' tae day wi' His Majesty."

"Ah read it , Ah'm tellin' ye," Annie reiterated.

"It's somethin' ye've read in a dentist's waitin' room," Andra said. He dismissed all references to any weakness in his hero's body.

"Did his hoarse hiv good teeth?" Hughie queried.

"They were perfect," Andra said, "When that hoarse smiled ye had tae put oan sun glesses."

"Imagine that!" Hughie was impressed.

"Anywey, teeth or no teeth, Oor Wullie up here wisnae a Scot."

"It disnae matter," Andra said, "there was loat o' the Scotch in him."

"Jist like you on a Setturday," Annie quipped.

"Ah still say Scots for the Scots," Andra grunted, "and Ah'm proud for tae be a native of this fair land," he sighed.

"Ah didnae know you were a native, Andra," Hughie said, surprised. "Ye don't even have a ring through yer nose."

"Don't talk so bloody stupit yae daft wee idiot," Andra said despairingly. "Ye can be a native without livin' in the jungle. You've been seein' too many Tarzan pictures."

"Aye, well," Annie sighed, "Ah'm gonny miss Mrs O'Reilly's company goin' doon tae the chapel. Such a nice quiet family. Ye don't know who you'll get in beside ye when a good neighbour leaves."

"Somebody wi' a road drill would be acceptable. No way can ye call the O'Reillys quiet. Whit aboot the time the auld granny died and they held a wake? The whole family a' staunin' roon the coaffin chantin' an' wailin'. Whit a racket! Ah had ta go in and tell them tae chuck it."

"Quite right." Hughie agreed.

"Too true," Andra said, "oor flute baun were tryin' tae practice that day. Couldnae hear oorsels for them next door."

"Some people are dead selfish," Hughie commiserated.

"You ur dead right, Hughie," Andra said.

"Er – whit exactly *is* a wake, Andra?" Hughie was puzzled.

"It's somethin' that you are no' usually, Hughie," Andra said facetiously.

"Don't you listen tae him," Annie said, sympathising with the wee man.

"They a' staun roon the coaffin, Hughie, makin' a racket jist hopin' that they'll waken up whoever's in that coaffin."

"Did it work wi' that auld wumman next door?" Hughie wanted to know.

"Hughie," Andra said, "Ah'm sure Ah saw that auld wumman sittin' up in that coaffin beltin' oot *Nellie Dean*. Either that or the priest was a ventriloquist. It's a wonder that the whole o' Dalbeth up the road wurnae a' sittin' up and joinin' in." Andra was referring to the Catholic cemetery just a few hundred yards up London Road – another reason for hating the site of his new home.

"Deid boadies shouldnae be daein' that, Andra," Hughie decided.

"Dead right, Hughie," Andra agreed. Suddenly, he felt the world was on top of him. He shuffled over to the picture of his hero. Looking up at the equestrian king he sighed. "How could you dae this tae me? Me, the loudest voice in Ibrox. Were ye getting' back at me for travellin' tae that infernal city, Rome? Well, it wisnae ma fault. It was daft Hughie's who bought a raffle ticket aff a wee nun. Ah know ye are no' pleased but ye didnae have tae go that faur – *twelve nothin*." Andra wept.

Hughie, seeing his pal's anguish, put a comforting arm around his heaving shoulder. "Here Big Man," he said, handing Andra what was left in the bottle.

Andra's eyes gleamed as he took the bottle. "Thanks, pal," he said. "It disnae help me forget that terrible tragedy but Ah'll try." Soon Hughie and Andra were having a session. Glasses clinked and, for a while, things got merrier.

"So, Ah take it that ye didnae like Ro . . . Ro . . . that place?" Hughie found it hard to say the word even though he now had enough liquid courage in him to bring up the subject. They had adjourned to the table and Annie, afraid that she might say something she would be sorry for, had retreated to the kitchen.

Andra took a large gulp from his glass. "Bloody awful, Hughie, so it was," he said, smacking his lips." Everywhere ye turn a' ye see is priests scurrying aboot. Ah had tae wear sun glesses – double glazing wans – tryin' tae avoid the sight."

"Geez, that was castrastonic, Andra, so it was," Hughie said. "But," he went on as an afterthought, "wis the drink dear?"

"*Drink!*" Andra scoffed. "They don't call it drink, Hughie. They drink stuff they call vino. Ye couldnae call it drink. Good for poalishin' furniture, aye, but no' for drinkin'. Ah telt Annie tae bring some hame for the sideboard."

"Whit a shame!" Hughie said.

"Ye want a drink tae put a shine oan *you* – no' the bloody sideboard," Andra said. "Even the weans drink it. Can ye imagine that happening' here, Hughie? A wee wean goin' intae the shoap and askin' for a bag-a-chips an' a tumbler o' furniture poalish."

"How did ye get oan wi' their money?" Hughie was curious.

"They call their money efter wan o' oor weans' gemmes. Ye know how we call oor money efter oor weights – pounds. They call theirs efter that gemme the weans play – wan, two, three a Leerie. No' only could Ah no' get tae grips wi' it but *they* were throwin' it away. Ah stood an' watched them daein' it. Couldnae believe ma eyes."

"Zat a fact?" Hughie could not believe his ears.

Just at that, Annie came in from the kitchen wiping her hands on her apron. "You canny talk aboot anybody, Andra," she said, "you throw yours away every other night doon at McDougall's."

"That's money well spent," Andra snapped.

"So, were ye jist walkin' alang the road and somebody passin' ye jist stuck their hauns in their poackets and threw their money away," Hughie was mesmerised.

"Naw, they threw it intae a fountain o' watter," Andra said.

"It's the Trevi Fountain, Hughie," Annie explained. "It's famous and ye're supposed tae throw yer coins in ower yer shooder and make a wish – and they say it means ye'll visit Rome again."

"Ah didnae throw any ma money," Andra said, screwing up his nose.

"Naw, you nearly got lifted for wadin' in and tryin' tae catch the money in an auld Marvel tin," Annie snapped. Her eyes went to the top of the sideboard and spotted a letter propped against a vase. Curious, she picked it up and examined the envelope. "It's for you," she said, passing it to Andra.

"Who could be sendin' me a letter?" he said, taking the envelope.

"Who knows ye can read?" Annie said sarcastically.

Andra ignored the remark.

"Maybe it's frae the Pope, Andra," Hughie said, "seein' ye made an impression oan him and oafferin' tae get him a season ticket for Ibrox."

"The *Pope!*" Annie burst out laughing. "Even the Devil widnae send *him* a letter," she chuckled.

Excitedly, Andra tore open the envelope and extracted the communication. He immediately went into raptures. Jumping up and down and waving the letter above his head, he cried: "It's frae the top man in the Holy Land . . . him himsel'."

"Ye . . . ye . . . mean it's frae . . ." Hughie stammered.

"Aye, it is," Andra said, proudly.

"It's frae God?" asked Hughie.

"Don't be so bloody stupit," Andra sniped. "It's frae somebody much mair important."

"Who could be mair important than God?" Annie snapped.

"Wullie Waddell," Andra said it almost in a whisper, referring to the manager of Rangers' Football Club.

"That's blasphemy," Annie said angrily. Comparing the Rangers manager with the Almighty was going too.

"So, who's yer letter frae?" Hughie asked.

"Ah jist telt ye," Andra said in despair. "The heid man in the Holy Land, Hughie, and that's Ibrox. It's frae the great Mr Waddell himsel' in person."

"And whit is the great Mr Waddell writin' tae you for?" Annie said in disbelief.

Andra did not answer. He was busy reading the great man's words. When he had finished, his jaw dropped. He let his arm fall to his side clutching the letter.

"Well?" Annie asked curiously.

"Ach, Ah've been turned doon again for ma request tae be buried in Ibrox Park," Andra grumbled. "Ah even telt them they didnae even hiv tae wait 'til Ah was deid."

"Whit aboot yer ashes, then?" Hughie piped up. "We could scatter them and it would save them diggin' a big hole in the field."

"No' even that, Hughie," Andra said glumly. "They said if they allowed that every supporter would want the same privilege and wi' the thousands of supporters they've got, the ashes would pile up. Wan gust o' wind and they'd get up everybody's nose."

"So, whit's new?" Annie said. "You dae that noo and ye're no' deid."

Andra was silent. Once more his greatest wish had been denied him. More than anything he wanted to lie in repose underneath the feet of his heroes. He had supported 'ra boys' ever since that day when his father carried him to see an old firm game. He was twenty-four at the time. He remembered how his father tossed his rickety into the air when Rangers scored a goal and how he threw *him* into the air when Celtic scored. From that day on he was hooked. He was enraptured with Rangers for the rest of his life. Green was for danger! He even refused to have greens on his plate and refused to dial *tim*, the speaking clock, when he wanted to know the time of day. He had tried every ruse he could to get noticed by the Rangers hierarchy, including chaining himself to the Ibrox goalpost and sending them poems composed by himself with the hope that he would be appointed the club's official bard. And he *was barred*. His lastest poem had been returned to him. He had put great hopes in this masterpiece, in his eyes it compared only to the efforts of Rabbie Burns, the national poet of Scotland. He would recite it word-for-word every night as he stood in front of the bathroom mirror before bed. It read:

> Youz are the greatest team wot Ah hiv ever seen,
> And mulk comes frae a coo,
> Ah'm gled that youz don't wear the green,
> But a lovely shade of blue.

Oh, yes, it was a masterpiece of great literary proportions. Alas, he received a reply from Mr Waddell himself. It read:

> We reject your little ode,
> It stinks just like an old commode,
> And if you think our hearts it melts,
> Bugger off and go to Celts.

Andra had contemplated suicide after that and taken a handful of paracetamol but all it did was keep him free of his rheumatism.

Andra's letter to the Ibrox Board was passed on to the Royal Infirmary Psychiatric Department.

* * *

Another great wish of Andra was to join the freemasons. A wish, too, that was denied him.

His great friend, Bowly McGeachie, a man of the world in Andra's eyes, had taught him some Masonic signs which, according to Bowly, assured him of being accepted into the Masons. Andra was beside himself with joy. Here was a way to make his mark in the world. Who knows who he might meet at these hallowed Masonic meetings. Even royalty were members. He wouldn't mind having a pint with the queen now and again.

Yes, he would have those who abandoned him – the supporters club, the "ludge". The Bridgeton Cross Communist Party, the Boy Scouts – all begging him to come and join their folds. The Rangers board would dig the hole themselves that would bury him at Ibrox Park. He would be a light in the community – a beacon of success.

On hearing that the local Masons were having a meeting, he saw his opportunity to go and get acquainted. He told Bowly his plans and Bowly gave him a warning not to blow it. The Masons were meeting at the Union of Catholic Mothers' hall that Wednesday night – the free night as the mothers would be away for a booze-up somewhere.

Bowly stressed to him that he must approach the head man with extreme caution and not be too pushy. So it was that Andra, disguised as a traffic warden, first class, sneaked his way in. Right away he spotted the Grand Master standing in deep conversation with a bunch of members. Andra quietly approached. Trying to attract attention to the Grand Master, he put his thumb to his nose and waggled it about (one of the signs that Bowly taught him meaning 'how do you do'). He patted his head twice, as Bowly had instructed and rolled his left trouser leg up.

Conversation stopped immediately and Andra was delighted. He had their attention. He stuck his fingers in his ears, stuck out his tongue and remembered the sacred words that had to be said. "Has your granny got a wart on her bum?" This was standard practice Bowly had assured him.

Andra picked himself up off the pavement, dusted himself down and wondered what he did wrong. He had done everything that Bowly had instructed. There would be other times!

The Orange Lodge had taken him on only because they were short of a base drum player. Andra had been recommended by a neighbour who was now completely deaf.

Andra was delighted that his musical talent was, at last, being recognised. He had thrown himself enthusiastically into his role and knew just when to raise the decibels as they passed by the chapel. He embarrassed his colleagues with his spitting bigotry and intolerance. He was not the calibre of Orangeman the lodge wanted – especially that day when the Grand Master picked up his *Daily Record* and saw Andra's picture plastered all over the front page. Andra had taken it upon himself to enhance the statue of the equestrian Duke of Wellington, which stood outside the Mitchell Library, in Queen Street, with an orange traffic cone He liked the colour and thought it would give the Duke a bit of added dignity. Unfortunately he had been spotted by a passing off-duty policeman who promptly arrested him and led him away by the scruff of the neck. The whole episode had been witnessed by a keen amateur photographer who had snapped the scene and sent it into the newspaper.

The minister attached to the Lodge found him intolerable. Especially as the poor man, trying to make himself heard as he gave his sermon to the gathering, was drowned out by Andra, sitting in the middle of the hall, practicing his big drum.

Andra was finally booted out of the Lodge. Too bigoted and racist was the reason given by the Grand Master. Andra could not believe how he, the most talented man in the entire 'ludge' could be expelled.

He decided that his "ludge" must really be a secret Catholic society. This would explain why the minister had asked him to muffle his drum

He had gone home that night, his chin on his chest, and poured out his heart to Annie. But he received no sympathy from his wife. She could now discard her ear plugs and, looking up, thanked God.

"Hell mend ye," she snapped. Annie had been embarrassed when she went shopping and saw her man's tortured face staring at her from every news stand. How could she face her fellow parishioners at Mass? Her 'chinas' at the weekly meeting of the liturgy group?

"You've been banned frae everything," she said angrily. "The Orange Ludge, the Rangers supporters, the Freemasons – ye showed yer ignorance tae that representative of the Brigton Croass Communist Party who came up tae the hoose tae vet ye for membership. Ye showed how ignorant ye are tae that wumman who came up, so ye did. Right away she telt ye that ye'd nae chance o' being' accepted – she knew just by lookin' at ye – ya ignorant get." Annie was on her high horse for all that she had a deep affection for her husband and tolerated his bigotry – as he tolerated her strong Catholic faith – just.

"Ach, that wumman was the ignorant get," Andra snapped. "She knew nothin' aboot communism – aboot how it a' started an' that. She had nae right bein' in the Party and haudin' the position she had. She knew nothin' aboot the great revolution of the revolvin' pheasants an' that. Of how it was the great Karl Marx that started it a' before he was joined by his brothers Groucho, Harpo and Chico – no' tae mention Gummo. And *she* had the gall for tae tear up ma application right in front o' me." Andra blew steam.

The whole world was against him. Head bowed, Andra stood before the picture of his hero and sadly shook his head. "*Twelve nothin!*" he groaned.

"Whit's it got tae dae wi' him?" Annie snapped.

"It's got everythin' tae dae wi' him," Andra retorted. "You've got the Pope, hiven't ye?"

"Aye, but he disnae play for Celtic," Annie snapped back adding, "and Oor Wullie there disnae play for Rangers. It's aboot time youse a' learned that – baith sides."

Andra did not want to hear his wife's tirade. Hughie poured out a couple of drinks and Andra downed his in a single gulp. He smacked his lips. "Nothin' else for it Hughie. If Sabastian has barred me frae the bus and Mr Waddell has stoaped me frae visitin' that holy ground, Ah will just have for tae go Incog . . . er . . . incog . . ."

"Incognizant," Hughie volunteered.

"Just whit Ah said." Andra coughed.

"Aye, it's a shame, Andra," Hughie said, shaking his head, "you will definitely no' be allowed oan the bus. Yer face is too well known. The boys in McDougall's would recognise yer badly marked face right away, so they wid."

"Ah hivnae got a badly marked face," Andra said, his hand coming up to his cheek.

"Ye wid if ye turned up at McDougall's," Hughie said with a straight face.

"Whit dae we dae, then?" Andra said worriedly.

"Ah'll tell ye whit we're *no*' daein," Hughie said. "We ur not goin' tae the gemme in Big Erchie's hearse again, so we're no'." Hughie shuddered.

"It got us here, didnt it?" Andra said.

"Ah don't like travellin' lyin' doon," Hughie said with a quiver. "Especially next tae a coaffin."

"Big Erchie was daein' us a favour," Andra said, "Don't forget oor bus was stolen. And, besides, whit herm did it dae lyin' next tae a coaffin? We were gonny get tae the promised land, that was the main thing."

"Ah nearly jumped oot ma skin Andra, when the body in the coaffin suddenly sat bolt upright and asked me for a light."

"Ach, that was Sammy McKenzie," said Andra dismissing Hughie's protest with a wave of the hand. "Erchie was gien him a lift as well."

"Aye, well Erchie should've telt us, so he should've," Hughie complained. "Ah thought it was Dracula," he went on, "Ah mean, Sammy is pasty-faced lookin' at the best o' times, int he?"

"Ah didnae know Dracula supported Rangers, "Annie said, chuckling.

Andra scowled at her."You haud yer weesh," he said. "Ah might be barred frae Ibrox but Ah will not hiv any derogat . . . er . . . derog . . . derogimanous remarks made aboot ra boys. The greatest fitba' team in the world – if no' elsewhere."

"Well, Ah don't care who Dracula supports," Hughie said. "Ah just don't like lyin' next tae a coaffin, so Ah don't. And, no' only that, this is a lovely hoose wi' it's ain lavvy an' that, but wi' two bad things connected wi' it."

"Whit two bad things are ye talkin' aboot?" Annie said angrily.

"Well, for wan thing," Hughie said, "youse are overlookin' Celtic Park."

"That's *eleven* bad things, " Andra said.

"And the other?" Annie asked, hands on hips.

"Well, them next door left because they saw a ghost," Hughie shivered.

"Whit ghost?" Annie said, knitting her brow.

"Ah don't know, "Hughie said, "but Ah thought Jean said it was a' in white."

"Long as it's no' green an' white," Andra said. "Ah'll no' staun for that."

"Ach, don't be daft!" Annie said.

"Whit dae ye mean 'don't be daft'," Andra snapped. "Ah canny have a green an' white ghost walkin' aboot the place. It's no' er – decorous."

"Ach, shut up," Annie replied. "Ye don't even know whit decorous means."

"Och, be fair, Annie," Hughie said. "Everybody knows whit that means."

"Right, then," Annie said, "you tell us."

"Aye, well – er – it means puttin' up wallpaper an' that!"

Annie threw her eyes towards heaven and sighed.

"Ah wull not have a green an' white cat in ma hoose never mind a wanderin' ghost," Andra said.

"Ye mean you're gonny take this snub?" Annie said. "You are still a Rangers fan despite them havin' nothin' tae dae wi' ye?"

"They might've gied me up but Ah will never gie them up,"

Andra said with a stiff upper lip. "Just as Ah will never gie up ma affi . . . er . . .affi . . . support o' the ludge, ma Masonic brothers or the Brigton Croass Communist Party – even though they have a dunderheid for a representative."

"If there's a dunderheid goin' aboot it's you, Andra," Annie said. "Can ye no' see that nane o' they organisations want anythin' tae dae wi' you and yer blinkers."

"Aye, well, you just wait, Annie," Andra said, raising his voice, "Ah'm gonny surprise you wan o' these days."

Annie noted the smug expression on her husband's face.

"Don't tell me ye're gonny get a joab?" she said in disbelief.

"Ah have somethin' special up ma sleeve that'll open a *lot* o' eyes," he said smugly."

"The only thing you've got special is a can o' Carlsberg in there, " Annie said facetiously, pointing towards the kitchen.

"Aye, well you just wait and see, "Andra said, pleased with himself. "Ah have been in commu . . . communi . . . touch wi' some powerful people and Ah'm just waitin' tae hear frae them – just you wait tae see me in ma new regalia, ma new uniform." Andra clicked his tongue.

Annie was not impressed and Hughie brought his eyebrows down, puzzled. "Uniform?" he said.

"The gear of a powerful organisation, Hughie," Andra said smiling.

"Ye've no' joined the Salvation Army, have ye?" Hughie asked sceptically.

"Don't be so stupit, ya we toad," Andra said. "Ma big drum is for wan marchin' baun only."

"The Sally Ann widnae have him anyway," Annie said. "Ye've burnt yer boats wi' the ludge, " she added, "ye should get that intae yer big bigoted heid."

"Ye think so, eh?"Andra said. "Well Ah'm tellin' ye ma boat will come in again."

Hughie had been thinking. Suddenly, he snapped his fingers. "Ah've got it ," he cried, "you're gonny be a sailor, is that it?"

"Honestly, Hughie, you ur the stupitist idiot Ah have ever known. Ye know Ah get seasick goin' tae Rothesay. Whit made ye think Ah was gonny be a sailor?"

"Boats – uniforms – get it? Ah just put two an' two the gether."

"Well ye'd better get back tae school," Andra sneered.

"Only wan thing he knows aboot boats is how tae push them oot," Annie said.

"Well, whitever it is, Ah canny wait for tae see ye in yer uniform, Andra," Hughie said eagerly.

"Nothin' tae dae wi' boats, ma wee man," Andra said. "Aye, it'll be somethin' for to behold," he added, puffing out his chest.

Something suddenly struck Hughie. "Here!" he exclaimed, "ye're jist back frae Ro . . . er . . . Ro . . ."

"*Rome*, Hughie – the word is *Rome*," Annie said angrily.

"Aye, right," Hughie said. "Ye – ye've no' been brainwashed have ye? Ye're no' becomin' a p . . . p . . . priest?"

"Not possible," Annie said, "ye need a brain tae be brainwashed."

Andra ignored his wife's remark. He turned to Hughie. "Don't be stupit ya wee elf," he said angrily, "how could Ah staun' up at Ibrox, bawlin' encouragement tae ra boys and at the same time suggestin' the Pope should feel the weight o' ma size nines. He would be ma boss, wint he?"

"Aye, right enough," Hughie said, after thinking about it. Then, with a cry of triumph, he said. "But that couldnae happen, Andra."

"How no'?" Andra snapped.

"'Cos you're banned frae Ibrox," Hughie said smugly.

"Och, that disnae count," Andra pooh-poohed, "they canny keep me away."

"Yer photay was plastered a' ower the *Daily Record*," Annie said, "and everybody doon at McDougall's knows ye – and it *is* their supporters' bus ye go on – ye've nae chance."

Andra dismissed his wife's comments with a wave of the hand. "Ra boys would miss ma voice if Ah wisnae there willin' them on tae victory," he said, "Ah'll disguise masel' and skip in. Ah'll need tae think up whit tae go as."

"Go as a normal human being," Annie volunteered. "They'll never recognise ye then."

"Very funny!" Andra said, "but Ah'll go and support the greatest team in the world – every wan o' they gods a good and true Scotsman as it should be and always will be."

"Ah widnae be so sure, Andra," Annie said. "Ye jist never know whit the future hauds."

"Naw, you're right, Andra," Hughie said. "Scots for the Scots."

"Aye, ye're tuned in, Hughie," Andra said.

Hughie smiled. He had pleased Andra. "And you watch whit yer sayin'," he said, turning to Annie.

"Ach, be quiet," Annie snarled.

"Ah hiv nae time for foreigners comin' here," he went on, "takin' oor joabs an' that."

Annie threw her head back. "Huh!" she said. "And when did anybody take your joab?"

"Some o' them say they are asylum seekers – escapin' frae dictators like that Idiot Amin bloke. But Ah don't believe that. Ah admit he's a big con man. Ah mean, Ah wance peyed ma subscription tae him for tae become a member o' their Uganda Masonic lodge. Then Ah found oot he was a Celtic supporter. Ah big con man so he is."

"Did ye get yer money back?" Hughie asked.

"That's nane o' your business," Andra said, embarrassed. "Jist send them a' hame," he said with determination.

Annie felt the steam rising within her. "These people have as much right tae be here for tae be happy and safe," she said angrily.

"How can they come here for tae be happy?" Andra said. "Ah stey here an' Ah'm no' happy."

"You widnae be happy in Paradise, Andra," Annie said.

"*Never*, but *never* mention that word in ma presence," Andra roared. Paradise, the name given to Celtic's stadium, in Parkhead, touched a raw nerve.

"Some o' they poor folk will be arrested and tortured, aye, and even killed, if they show their faces back in their ain country," Annie went on.

"That's right, Andra," Hughie said.

"You shut yer face," Andra snapped. "Ye canny get arrested for jist showin' yer face – although *you* could."

"Oh, and is that so?" Annie said, hands on hips. "Jist whit did that Italian polis say tae you when he escorted ye oan tae the plane?"

Andra thought for a moment. "He said somethin' aboot

somebody called Erchie and Ah telt him that wisnae ma name and that he'd got the wrang bloke," Andra said.

"He said nothin' o' the kind," Annie said. "Arriverderci – nothin' tae dae wi' anybody called Erchie – and he said, 'don't ever let me see your face here again'."

"Ach, foreigners," Andra grumbled, "Ah couldnae understaun a word he was sayin."

"He couldnae understaun a word *you* were sayin'," Annie retorted. "In fact," she went on, "Ah couldnae understaun a word you were sayin'."

"Ach, away wi' ye," Andra said dismissively.

"Ye gave me nothin' but a red face a' the time we were in Rome, ya ignorant get." She snapped. "Nae wonder Rangers want nothin' tae dae wi' ye."

"Whit did Ah ever dae tae gie ye a red face?" Andra said, hurt.

"Whit aboot that time we were goin' tae the Vatican and a big notice said that men enterin' were not allowed tae wear shorts," Annie said grimly.

"Whit aboot it?" Andra asked, knitting his brow.

"It didnae mean takin' them aff and enterin' in yer Y-fronts. Yer attitude was reprehen . . . er . . . repr . . ."

"Representative is the word you're lookin' for," Hughie said.

"Reprehensible is the word," Annie said, "and it's no' strong enough."

"Ach, ye're nit pickin'," Andra said.

"Aw, Derbac soap's good for that," Hughie blurted out. "Ma maw used tae get stuck intae ma heid wi' the old Derbac and a fine-tooth comb." Hughie was pleased that he could contribute to the conversation.

"Shut yer geggie you," Andra snapped. "She is just lookin' for excuses."

"Tae examine your heid? " Hughie said in disbelief.

"Your maw definitely did some herm tae your heid wi' a' her proddin ya wee hauf-wit," Andra said.

"Ma maw's deid," Hughie said sadly.

"And Ah'm no' nit-pickin'." Annie said. "If ma face had been any redder they'd be callin' me Pochahuntas."

"Whit's a Welsh singer got tae dae wi' anything?" Andra said, puzzled.

"Ya ignorant get," Annie replied scornfully. "Ye nearly got us arrested as well."

"When?" Andra drew down his brows.

"That time ye went ower tae that car wi' the word *carabiniere* printed oan the side o' it."

"So, whit was wrang wi' that?" Andra protested.

"Ye asked for a plate o' spaghetti and and the big polis thought ye were takin' the mickey," Annie said.

"It was an honest mistake," Andra said. "Ah thought it was a street trader sellin' spaghetti – jist like ye get Tally ice-cream vans goin' aboot. We've a' heard o' spaghetti carabiniere, int we?"

"Spaghetti *carbonara*, Annie corrected, "*carabiniere* mean the polis, ya clown."

"Ah guessed Ah'd made a mistake when that big cop behind the wheel jist stared at me and showed me his teeth," Andra said.

"Whit did ye dae?" Hughie asked.

"Ah telt him they were very nice and haunded them back," Andra said with a straight face.

"Ach, well, ye're hame noo among yer ain folk, Andra," Hughie said, slapping his back.

"Aye, some folk," Andra said sadly. "Hughie, dae ye really think that Sabastian an' ra boys don't like me?"

"Well, Big Sabastian telt me that, personally, he didnae dislike ye."

Andra's eyes brightened. He saw a glimmer of hope. "He said that?" he beamed.

Hughie nodded. "He telt me that himsel. He telt me that doon in McDougall's."

"Whit did he say, Hughie? Tell me – tell me." Andra asked excitedly.

Hughie cleared his throat. "He telt me doon in McDougall's," Hughie began.

"Whit he say, whit he say," Andra was shaking with excitement.

Hughie went on. "He said he didnae dislike ye – he hated ye. He said he wanted for tae get rid o' ye wance and for all."

Andra's jaw dropped. "Whi . . . whit does he hate me for?" he stammered.

"He says yer singin' oan the bus puts everybody aff," Hughie said.

43

"Ah jist sing as loud as everybody else," Andra was hurt.

"But Danny Boy isnae wan o' oor songs, Andra," Hughie said.

Andra grabbed Hughie by the throat and shook him violently. "Ya wee nyaff," he cried, "ye're makin' this up, so ye are, int ye?"

"Ah'm no', Andra, Ah'm no'," the wee man gasped.

Annie stepped in and pulled her husband off Hughie, whose face was turning blue.

"Stoap it – stoap it, "she yelled. "Look – his face is turnin' blue.."

"Well, it's the right colour anyway," Andra said, releasing his grip.

Hughie ran his finger under his collar and took a deep breath. "It wisnae me that said it, Andra, it was Sabastian," he choked.

"Ah know, Ah know, Hughie," Andra said, feeling contrite, "Ah'm sorry, Ah got cerried away."

"Aye, that's another thing that happened in Rome," Annie grumped.

"Whit are ye talkin' aboot?" Andra snapped.

"Mind that day ye went up tae that Swiss Guard and asked him for two tickts tae the matinee? Ah had tae hide ma face," Annie shook her head.

"Ye don't dae that oaften enough," Andra said facetiously.

Annie ignored him. "Ah was fair ashamed," she said.

"Ah thought he was dressed up for Aladdin or somethin'," Andra said.

"Ye got cerried away that day and slung right oot the door. Again ye were just showin' yer ignorance. You are a bigot, Andra – a bigot and a racist." Annie dabbed her eye.

"Ah am nut a bigot or a racist," Andra protested. "Ah am the maist toler . . .tol . . . intolerable man ye ever met, so Ah am. Ah am nut ignorant. Ah was number wan in English, so Ah was."

"*YOU!* Number wan in English?" Annie cried incredulously, throwing up her arms.

"Aye, *Me*," Andra said, hurt. "Ah could rhyme aff every team in the English First Division."

"Fitba'! That's your religion, Andra. Ye're blinkered. It's yer only conversation. If there was nae fitba' in this world your mooth would never be opened." Annie was getting angrier.

"Ye're talkin' rubbish, Annie, so ye ur," Andra sniped.

"Even that wee priest wee met oan the piazza and you refused tae shake hauns wi' him – even then ye had tae bring fitba' intae the conversation."

"Whit did Ah say?" Andra was flummoxed.

"When he said he was goin' in search of the Holy Grail – the cup used at the Last Supper – you telt him he was wastin' his time and that *you* knew where it was. The wee man's face lit up. Ah watched his eyes brighten. 'Where?' he asked a' excited – 'In Rangers' trophy room,' you said."

"Well, tae me, the Scottish Cup *is* the Holy Grail," Andra retorted, "And, for your information," he added, "Ah did not shake hauns wi' him because he was ignorant and obviously didnae want tae shake hauns wi' me."

"Don't be ignorant," Annie said, "he held oot his haun tae ye and ye looked away. Ah was ashamed."

"He is the ignorant wan," Andra said. "He was wearin' gloves."

"A loat o' people wear gloves," Annie said.

"No' oven gloves Annie," Andra replied smugly.

"Maybe he'd come straight frae the kitchen," Hughie said. "Maybe he was cookin' somethin'."

"Like ma goose, maybe, "Andra said. "Ye canny be up tae them, Hughie. They're oot for tae convert ye every chance they get. That wee priest didnae bother Annie, jist me. He could tell that she was already wan o' them."

"How could he tell, Andra?" Hughie asked.

"She had a statue o' St Christopher roon her neck," Andra replied.

"Loats o' women have a statue o' St Christopher – the patron saint o' travellers – roon their necks," Annie protested.

"No' six feet tall marble wans they don't," Andra said.

"So, how did he know that you wurnae a pape, Andra?" Hughie was interested.

"Ah don't know, Hughie," Andra said. "Ah had ma Rangers gear oan right enough – just like in that photay up there."

Andra pointed to a picture of himself alongside King William, astride his famous horse, at the battle of the Boyne in 1690. Andra wore a blue and white 'title' hat with matching woollen scarf and a four-foot in diameter rosette in the team's colours.

"Aye, ye couldnae miss him – walkin' aboot the piazza – like a walkin' advert for Ibrox. And that reminds me," she added, taking Andra's coveted picture down from the wall and replacing it on the reverse side where the picture of Pope Pius the Tenth smiled down on the gathering.

"It's *ma* turn tae have His Holiness showing."

She took a step back, surveyed *her* coveted picture and smiled.

"Hey!" Andra cried, "It's no' the end o' the month when you can put up Gunga Din there. That's whit we agreed."

"We agreed tae nae such thing," Annie protested. "We agreed that if Rangers got beat Ah would be allowed tae put His Holiness up and if Celtic got beat –"

She didn't finish.

"So," Andra said, "When did the boys get beat, eh? We've been away."

"*Twelve nothin'*, Andra, remember?" Annie said with glee.

"Aw, that disnae count," Andra wailed, "Ah wisnae here for tae shout ma support."

"Aye, it counts, Andra," Annie chuckled. "And up there he steys."

"An agreement's an agreement, Andra," Hughie said.

"You shut yer face," Andra said angrily.

Hughie just shrugged. He was used to Andra's moods. But he was a loyal friend and would never mention a word to the boys down in McDougall's that true-blue Andra had a picture of the Pope up on his wall.

"You shut yer eyes – *and* yer mooth," Andra snapped at Hughie. "This is nut a sight for innocent eyes like yours. And ye don't want for tae be attendin' the Eye Infirmary, in Berkeley Street, dae ye?"

Hughie shook his head vigorously.

"Wan word o' this, "Andra said, pointing his finger into the wee man's face, "an' you wull be attendin' the Orthopaedic department at the Royal Infirmary, wi' a broken leg an' that – right?"

Hughie nodded more vigorously.

Andra turned towards the picture of his hero. "Your Majesty," he began, "Ah am sorry that you have for to be subjected to this indignity – for to be up there alongside this – er – this – mafia chieftain while Ah am turned tae the wa'. But Ah swear on John

Knox's hallowed grave that Ah wull release you as soon as possible."

"Listen tae him," Annie said scornfully, "talkin' tae a hoarse."

"Ah am nut talking tae the hoarse," Andra snapped. "Ah am talkin' tae His Majesty."

"Oh, aye," Annie said and turned away.

*   *   *

"Hiv ye seen yer new neighbour yet?" Hughie inquired.

"Don't be so bloody stupit,"Andra said, "sure we're just hame frae that sufferin' hoaliday you fixed for me. Ah didnae know we had new neighbours."

"Oh, aye, intae the O'Reillys' hoose they are. Ah wonder if they've seen the ghost, yet?" Hughie shivered once more.

"Ghosts, toasts," Andra scoffed. "If you don't shut up *you'll* be seein' ghosts – in fact you'll be wan o' them."

"Ah helped them up wi' their stuff," Hughie said.

"Aw, that was very neighbourly of ye Hughie," Annie said.

"Whit kinda stuff?" Andra was curious.

"They had a big trunk –" Hughie began.

"Was there an elephant attached tae it?" Andra asked facetiously.

Hughie shook his head, wondering why anybody would have an elephant as a pet.

"Thank God for that!" Andra said, "At least they're no' frae the Punjab."

"Never you mind him," Annie said. "You were bein' friendly Hughie."

After thinking it over, Andra shrugged.

"Ach, well," he said, "they couldnae be any worse neighbours than them O'Reillys – a' that chantin' an' that."

"People are people, Andra," Annie said. "It disnae matter whit race, creed or colour ye are. We are a' Jock Tamson's bairns."

"Aye, but we're no' a' *Andra* Tamson's bairns. Ah don't want any o' them foreigners up here. Ah've got nae time for them – comin' here an' taken the joabs aff o' us citizens." Andra nodded. He agreed with himself.

"*Work?*" *Work?*" Annie cried, throwing up her arms. "When did you ever work?"

"It's ma back," Andra complained, bending backwards and rubbing his back.

"Ye should try some Deep Heat, Andra," Hughie volunteered.

"He'll get plenty o' that when he snuffs it," Annie said cattily.

"Ah'm goin' tae heaven when Ah go," Andra said. "Six Feet under the Ibrox turf, that's where Ah'll be." He smiled broadly. He couldn't wait. "That Rangers board will come aroon' wan day an' realise ma worth and ma years o' devotion."

"Like a pig's arse, they will," Annie scoffed. "Are they nice people, Hughie – them that's moved in next door?"

"Oh. Aye, they looked nice and respectable," Hughie said.

"Just as long as they're no' foreigners," Andra said. "We don't want any o' them asylum seekers skivin aff us."

"Whit dae ye mean 'skivin'?" Annie cried.

"The first thing they ask when they get here is how tae get tae the benefit oaffice – that is skivin', hen," Andra snapped.

"Rubbish!" Annie retorted.

A sudden burst of *The Sash My Father Wore* pealed from the doorbell.

"Ah'll get it," Annie said, heading for the door. Voices could be heard from the lobby and Annie finally came in accompanied by the newcomer. "Andra, this is oor new neighbour who's come tae introduce himsel'."

Andra let his glass drop and shatter. Standing there with outstretched hand was a six-foot tall black African man, his pure white teeth flashing a dazzling smile.

"How do you do, Mr Thomson," he smiled.

"Get oot," Andra snapped.

"He'll dae nae such thing," Annie said angrily. "Come away in and sit yersel' doon."

"Are you daft?" Andra sniped.

"Naw, it's you that's daft," Annie said.

"Hello!" the new neighbour said. "I am Wullie McNab and I am very pleased to meet you."

Andra stuck his hands in his pockets and Wullie withdrew his hand when he saw it was not going to be taken.

"Wullie McNab?" Andra said, his brows coming down. "How the hell can you have a good Scots name like that?"

"My father was a Scottish soldier serving in Uganda when he met my mother," Wullie said.

"So, away back," Andra said.

"*Andra!!*" Annie snapped angrily.

"I am seeking asylum here in the land of my father," Wullie said.

"Well, if it's asylum ye want ye've come tae the right hoose," Annie said. "This is as near tae an asylum as you'll get."

"Have ye nae asylums in yer ain country?" Andra asked.

"I and my family are fleeing from Idi Amin, who is a tyrant."

"Aye, Ah've heard o' him," Andra said. "Idi, it's shoart for Idiot, int it?"

"You are Andrew, right?"

"*Andra*," Andra said. "Don't tell me your here wi' yer hale family?"

"Oh yes," Wullie said. "Me, my wife, Bronwyn."

"Don't tell me she's Irish?" Andra said.

"Bronwyn's father was a Welsh missionary," Wullie said. "He, too, has vanished from Amin's terror."

"Are ye sure youse didnae eat him?" Andra said.

"*Andra!!!*" Annie bawled.

Wullie shrugged. His eyes went to the picture of King Billy on the wall. "Ah, I see you are an equestrian man," he said.

"Ah am not!" Andra said adamantly. "Ah know nothin' aboot swimmin'."

"I meant you like horses," Wullie said.

"Oh, aye, he's never oot o' William Hill's shoap," Annie said.

"You work with horses, Andrew?" Wullie inquired, showing interest.

"Ah don't work because o' ma bad back," Andra said, "and ma name's *Andra* but you call me Mister – Mister Sinatra."

"That's no' yer name," Annie snapped.

"Ah know, but Ah like it," Andra said.

"Don't forget it's an Italian name," Annie reminded him.

"Geez, Ah never thought o' that," Andra grimaced. "Well, ye can call me Mister Proddy."

"That's no' yer name either," Annie said despairingly.

"You will be on benefit, then, with you having the bad back, eh?" Wullie asked.

"*Benefit?*" Andra bawled out the word. "Ah've never been oan benefit."

Annie threw her eyes heavenwards.

"Ah don't even know where the benefit oaffice is," he went on.

Wullie took Andra by the elbow and led him to the window. Pointing, he said, "See that building with the red roof? Well, that is the benefit office, go in and ask for Wee Sammy. He is the chief clerk and is a very nice man. Sammy has a wife, called Maisie and has two weans."

Andra's mouth fell. "Ye don't happen tae know whit she gies him for his piece, dae ye?"

"Yes," Wullie said. "Usually cheese and onion. He likes that."

Andra did not see Wullie winking at Annie. He had Andra well sussed and thought he would wind him up. Annie smiled and nodded. Yes, she'd got the picture.

Andra was gobsmacked. "Geez!" he groaned. "He probably even knows whit the linoleum in there is like."

"They have a blue Axminster carpet," Wullie said, winking once more at Annie who hid a wide smile. "Well, I must get back to my dear wife and our children." Wullie turned towards the door.

"Er – how many weans have ye got?" Andra asked.

"Two," Wullie said, "Osama and Saddam. I see them making a name for themselves in this world."

"Only if they become fitba' players," Andra said.

"You never know," Wullie said, "one day they could be playing for Celtic." Once more he winked over at Annie. Yes, Wullie could see right through Andra and he was just the man who would not let him get away with his racism. With a cheery wave, Wullie closed the door quietly behind him.

"Well, he looks a really nice man," Annie said.

Andra was not happy. He grabbed Hughie by the back of the neck and led him towards the door.

"Away you go home," he ordered, "and keep yer trap shut aboot *him*." Andra jabbed his thumb towards the Pope's picture.

One shove and Hughie was out on the landing.

Andra flopped on to the couch. He suddenly felt weary. It was a long flight with Andra higher than the plane for most of the journey. When his head hit the pillow that night Wullie's face kept appearing in front of him. He buried his head in the soft pillow but, despite his tiredness, sleep evaded him.

He could hear the ghostly voices of the inhabitants of Dalbeth, the Catholic cemetery just up the road repeating:

"*Twelve-Nothing . . . Twelve-Nothing!*"

CHAPTER THREE

STRONG SUNLIGHT STREAMING THROUGH THE WINDOW AND A loud, authoritative rapping at the door had Andra pulling the pillow over his ears.

He turned and glanced at the bedside clock. The illuminated hands told him it was 7.30 a.m. Who could be battering at his door at this time, he wondered, and why had they not used the doorbell? He would not have minded the intrusion into his sleep had he woken to the musical sound of his favourite chimes.

Annie, too, was awakened by the rapping on the door. She jumped up, slipped into a dressing gown and opened the door. The postman handed her a brown paper parcel and a letter. She made a quick perusal of the parcel. It was addressed to Mr Andrew Thomson of the Rangers and the letter was addressed to both of them. She clasped the letter to her chest. Yes, it was Peter's handwriting.

Andra was now out of bed. He wandered into the room scratching his sleepy head, threw open the window and took a deep breath. "Ah," he sighed, "smell that good Scottish air . . . no' a whiff of garlic. Aye, it's great tae be hame."

Annie threw the parcel on to the table. "That's for you," she said, curious to know what it contained.

Andra pounced on it and perused the post mark with an excited eye. "It . . . it's frae America," he whooped, "the land o' that great Rangers supporter, John Wayne."

"Ach, yer granny," Annie retorted. "He's probably never heard o' the Rangers, same as him," Annie jabbed her thumb towards the picture of the King.

"Whit dae ye mean, 'never heard o' Rangers'?" Andra snapped. "*Everybody* has heard o' Rangers."

"John Wayne hisnae," Annie said.

"Aye he has," Andra said angrily, "he was even in a picture a' aboot them."

"Whit picture was that?" Annie scoffed.

"The Texas Rangers," Andra replied with a smug expression.

"They were cowboys," Annie said, "nothin' tae dae wi' the Rangers fitba' team."

"Aye, they were," Andra argued. "they were always talkin' aboot Billy."

"Aye, Billy the Kid," Annie said. "Ah'm beginnin' tae get worried aboot you, Andra. Ah don't think you're the full shullin', ye're no' even tenpence ha'penny."

"Ah am so tenpence ha'penny," Andra said.

Annie *was* worried. Andra's blinkers were getting thicker.

"Right then," she said. "Tell us whit's in the parcel?"

Andra clasped the parcel closer to his chest. "That is ma secret," he said, "but Ah'm assumin' it's ma regalia, ma uniform." Andra would keep Annie and Hughie in the dark until he was good and ready to let them into his secret.

Annie shrugged. "Please yersel'," she said nonchalantly.

Annie retreated to the kitchen and Andra scurried into his bedroom. Frantically he tore at the wrapping. His eyes widened with excitement as he removed the garment and held it up at arm's length to get a better look at it. He was surprised that such an august body had styled their regalia in this unusual pattern. But they knew what they were doing, he was sure of that. He held the garment close to his body, surveyed himself in the long mirror, clicked his tongue against his cheek. Yes, he was quite pleased with himself. Let the local Masons keep him out now. And that went for the Supporters' Club, the 'Ludge' and the rest of them. He heard the door handle being turned and quickly bundled up his prize and chucked it under the bed.

Andra, whistling his favourite tune, was standing innocently looking towards the ceiling as Annie burst in waving the letter.

"It's frae Peter," she cried with delight.

"And whit is Saint Peter sayin'?" Andra asked sarcastically.

"He's comin' hame for a hoaliday frae the seminary," Annie gushed. "He's comin' for two weeks. Isn't that marvellous?"

"Ah'll dust aff ma halo," Andra said.

Peter's visit was just one more embarrassment for Andra. He had managed to keep his son out of sight of the McDougall clan the last time he arrived home.

Annie remembered Andra's antics during that visit. How

Andra introduced Peter to some of his pals he couldn't avoid by saying the boy was appearing as Friar Tuck in the Pavilion Theatre's Robin Hood pantomime.

"Noo, Ah'm warnin' you, Andra," Annie growled, pointing a finger. "*You* gie that boy the respect he deserves when he comes hame, hear me?"

Andra, head bowed, said nothing. He knew better than to argue with Annie. He knew how proud she was that their son had not only joined her church but had done a complete conversion somersault and had gone off to a seminary to study for the priesthood. Andra wondered where *he* had gone wrong? Hadn't he taught Peter all he knew – how to swear in foreign languages in case his team went to Europe?

But his son had shown no interest. It was Annie, the devout Catholic, who had nibbled at Peter's ear, he was sure of that. At first Peter had tried to compromise with his father for the sake of peace. Andra was stunned one day when he walked into his son's room and saw a framed picture of the great reformer, John Knox, on the wall wearing a Celtic football strip. He had managed to keep Peter's flight from the faith from his cronies down at McDougall's. But Peter, himself, was not one to hide his new allegiance and that was Andra's worry. He would have to face that when he came to it.

"Two weeks is a bit long, is it no'?" he said, grimacing.

"It's no' long enough," Annie said, smiling.

"Aye, well, jist keep him in the hoose," Andra said, "Ah don't want him paradin' up an' doon the street wearin' that Friar Tuck gear you bought him."

"Have ye ever looked at some o' the gear *you* wear?" Annie sniped.

"That's different," Andra said.

"Aye, well you just remember whit Ah said," Annie went on. "Gie the boy the respect he deserves."

"Ah'll gie him whit he deserves, a'right," Andra rasped. He avoided eye contact with his wife and did not see the contemptuous look she threw at him.

* * *

54

"Did ye know we found the bus, Andra." said Hughie, later that morning.

"Where?" Andra's brows went up.

"Ootside the chapel wi' a photay o' the Pope in the drivin' seat," Hughie said.

"Ye canny be up tae them, eh!" Andra said, shaking his head.

"Sabastian was jist pleased that they'd fun' it. Ah mean we need it for goin' tae Manchester on Setturday."

"Whit's happenin' in Manchester?" Andra asked.

"We're playin' Manchester United," Hughie said, wondering how Andra didn't know.

Andra slapped his forehead.

"Geez!" he said, "Ah nearly forgot aboot that. Wi' a' this goin' oan. Just back frae that place. Saint Peter comin' hame. Al Jolson movin' in next door – *twelve nothin'* – it's been some day!"

"It's a shame ye'll no' be there, Andra," Hughie commiserated.

"Oh, Ah'll be there, son. Ah'll be there," Andra said with determination.

"No' on the bus, ye'll no'," Hughie said.

"There's mair than wan wey tae skin a cat, Hughie," Andra said.

"Ye takin' a baldy cat wi' ye – that'll no' help," Hughie said.

"Ah am nut takin' a baldy cat wi' me," Andra said despairingly. "That's just a sayin', Hughie."

Andra was sad that Sabastian had barred him from the bus. They had been good friends at one time. In fact Andra had taken Sabastian's little daughter, Mary-Teresa, to Blackpool on her sixth birthday for a treat – along with Annie, Jean and Peter. Unfortunately, he lost her. She just wandered off and was never seen again. Sabastian was not pleased but they remained friends until the little girl turned up ten years later. Andra thought Sabastian would be over the moon as they were re-united. Instead he had a heart attack and had to be resuscitated. Andra reckoned it was the Mother Superior habit she was wearing that caused Sabastian's sudden stroke.

"C'mon Hughie," Andra said, "you and me are goin' doon for a pint."

Hughie's eyes lit up. "We canny go tae McDougall's," he said.

"There are other pubs," Andra replied.

They left and Annie gave a long sigh. She was glad to see the back of her husband for a while.

★   ★   ★

The barman of the *Hare and Hounds* was wiping the bar when the pair entered.

"Don't usually see you staunin' at ma bar," he said to Andra.

"Whit dae ye mean?" Andra said.

"Ah mean Ah don't usually see you staunin' period," the man said.

"Ur you bein' funny?" Andra said aggressively.

"Naw, naw," the barman said, holding up his palm. "Jist surprised, that's a'. You're a McDougall's customer, int ye?"

"It's gettin' done up the noo," Andra lied.

"Aye, Ah thought Ah saw the painter goin' there wi' his green paint," the man said.

Their eyes met and both burst out laughing.

"So, whit ye have?" the barman asked.

"Ah'll hiv a Guinness," Hughie said.

Andra choked. "Put yer haun oan that counter, Hughie," he said.

"Eh?" Hughie said, puzzled.

"The counter," Andra said, nodding towards the bar.

Hughie shrugged and complied.

His hand stung as Andra's fists came down on it.

"Hey!" the wee man shouted, blowing into his hand.

"Don't you ever let me hear you swearin' again," Andra warned. "Two haufs and two hauf pints," he ordered.

The pair retired to a corner table with their refreshments.

"So, ye think ye'll get tae the gemme in Manchester, Andra?" Hughie said when they were settled.

"You wull hear ma voice, Hughie, don't worry," Andra said.

"Dae ye think we can beat them?" Hughie said.

"We can beat *anybody*, Hughie," Andra said. "We've got God oan oor side."

"Whit position is he playin', Andra?" Hughie asked.

"They are a' gods, Hughie – every wan," Andra replied.

★   ★   ★

Andra left Hughie and headed home. Besides money was short after their Roman sojourn.

Annie was serving tea and biscuits to Wullie and Bronwyn when Andra entered. He stopped in his tracks. Bronwyn was wearing the traditional burka completely covering her face, which she would raise to sip her tea. Pointing a shaking finger at his new neighbours, Andra could not contain himself.

"Whit's Sabu daein' here," he bawled, "and wi' the Lone Ranger as well?"

Annie flushed. "You shut yer mouth," she said sharply. "Ye must be neighbourly. Wullie got a very discouragin' letter frae the Home Office today. They might be turnin' doon his application an'deportin' him," she added.

"An' his weans as well?" Andra's eyes brightened.

"Them a'." Annie said, passing the biscuits.

"Ah'll see them tae the boat," Andra said gleefully, adding, "Ah mean youse come here, youse have nae skills and right away no' only dae ye know the wee man in the benefits oaffice, ye know whit he gets for his dinner."

"But Bronwyn does have skills," Wullie said. "She is an obstetrician and I have a degree in Archaeology."

"Andra's got an 'ology' as well," Annie piped up.

"Oh! In what may I ask?" Wullie said curiously.

"In *alchoh – ology*," Annie said with a wry smile.

Wullie and Bronwyn laughed.

"So you ur good wi' the bow an arra," Andra said to Wullie. "There urnae many joabs goin' aboot for Archae . . . wan o' them things," Andra said. "And Ah canny see much work goin aboot for an obstetrician, either. Maist folks have good eyesight and don't need glesses."

Annie threw Andra one of her famous 'looks'.

Bronwyn continued sipping her tea in her usual fashion.

"Would ye look at that!" Andra cried. "She's tae lift that curtain everytime she wants a drink."

"It's our custom," Wullie said. "The women must wear the burka and cover their face."

"Ah wish the custom would catch on here," Andra said, glancing at Annie who sat scowling. "Aye, the Home Office is right for tae send youse hame," Andra went on. "You asylum seekers come here and take oor joabs because youse know we're a saft touch – and there's naebody as saft as me – anybody wull tell ye. Even oor illustrious chairman o' ma Orange Ludge telt me Ah was the saftest man he'd ever met *and* Ah was touched as well. Ye don't get any better recommendations than that." Andra was proud of himself.

Wullie had met Andra's type before and said nothing. Better to let him rant on and get it out of his system.

"It was bad enough hivin' them yins next door without youse lot," Andra went on. "The stairheid used tae smell o' incest sticks frae that walkin' blanket and cabbage frae they midget priests across the landin'. Noo, Ah suppose, it'll smell o' curry. It's just too much!" Andra shook his head.

"What would you rather it smelled of?" Wullie said.

"Mince an' totties, whit else," Andra sniffed and sighed. "An' maybe a black puddin' supper an' that." He smacked his lips.

"I think you are a racist and a bigot, Mr Thomson," Wullie said.

"*Me? a racist and a bigot?*" Andra blurted. "Annie. Tell 'im – am no' Ah a bigot? Go on tell 'im."

Annie came round the table and, standing behind her husband, put her hands on his shoulders.

"Andra," she said, "You think that Songs of Praise should include Follow Follow We Wull Follow Rangers."

"*That* is just musical preference," Andra protested.

"What's that tune your doorbell plays?" Wullie asked, though he knew the answer. "Isn't that *The Sash My Father Wore*?"

"So what?" Andra said. "Ah suppose you've got tom-toms playin'."

Wullie merely smiled. Yes, Andra was true to form.

"Look," Andra went on, "youse foreigners are no' wanted here. No' only do Ah hate youse interlopers, Ah even hate some o' ma ain Scotsmen – they ur called Celtic supporters. But at least they sit oan chairs when they eat."

"I am sitting on a chair," Wullie protested.

"Only because ye're in *ma* hoose," Andra said."Back in yer ain country youse a' squat on the mud – a' stickin' yer hauns intae cocy-nut shells full o' deid monkey. Youse have never heard o' knives an' foarks – barbaric, so it is. Youse have nae table manners – and that's because youse have nae tables."

"I take it that you never eat with your fingers, Mr Thomson?"

"*Never!*" Andra cried.

Annie glanced towards heaven.

"Noo, Andra," she said. "Tell the truth, you hiv been known tae use yer fingers."

"*When?*" Andra said angrily. "Tell me when Ah have ever ate like these unwashed?" Andra did not like Annie taking this asylum seeker's part.

"Every Setturday night when ye leave McDougall's, stoap in at Mario's and stagger up the street feedin' yer face wi' a fish supper – ye're a' fingers then." Annie rubbed it in.

"*That* is different," Andra said. "That is the great Glesca ritual."

Wullie rose and, taking Bronwyn's arm, turned at the door. To Annie he said, "Thank you for your kind hospitality, Mrs Thomson, and may God bring peace to this house."

"He'll need tae bring a squadron of angels alang wi' 'im," Annie said.

Andra was glad to see his new neighbours depart.

"Aye, away ye go," he said, "and ye canny be much o' an obstat . . . wan o' them things when yer ain eyes must be in some state." Pointing at Bronwyn, he went on, "If ye were any good at yer joab how could ye mairry her. She must've some coupon when ye have tae hide it behind that pelmet."

"I admit I do have a cataract," Wullie said.

"Ah am nut a bit interested in yer boat," Andra snapped. "Noo away and join yer ghost."

"What ghost?" Wullie queried.

"Ma pal Randy of incest stick fame," Andra said. "He haunts your hoose and may he stink it – and you oot."

"You have a friend in the other world?" Wullie asked.

"Ah have nae freens in the Celtic supporters' club," Andra said.

"He hasnae even any freens in the *Rangers* supporters' club," Annie said.

"No, I mean in the spirit world," Wullie said.

"Oh, he's got plenty there," Annie said, "Johnny Walker, Jack Daniels, Jim Beam – no' forgettin' the Bells family."

"Aye, ma freen, Randy, is daein ma work for me – frightenin' people. He got rid o' that Irish crowd next door, dint he – and wi' any luck Ah'll get rid o' you and Old Mother Riley, there."

Wullie laughed. "There are no' such things as ghosts," he said. "When we die we are judged and then get sent to Heaven or Hell. If we are good we can enter Paradise."

"Hey, watch yer language," Andra said.

"And if we're bad we are despatched to hell. What do you know about hell?"

"Twelve nothin'," Andra groaned. "Noo, get oot – and if Maria Montez there is gonny make ye a curry, make sure yer windaes are open." With that he shoved them out and slammed the door.

"You were a bit nasty tae him," Annie scolded.

"He's a foreigner," Andra snapped, "he shouldnae be here."

"Whit have ye got against foreigners?" Annie, said, hands on hips.

"They ur foreign," Andra replied sourly.

"Whit would ye say if hauf yer Rangers team was made up of foreigners?"

"*That* wull never happen," Andra said.

Annie nodded towards the picture of the King. "Ah'll remind ye again," she said, "Billy the Kid up there is a Dutchman – noo ye canny say *he's* no a foreigner."

"You will refrain frae callin' His Majesty Billy the Kid or any other derog . . . derog . . . bad names," he snapped. "Besides, his hoarse was brought up in Larkhall and they baith learned how tae swim in the Clyde for their forthcomin' crossin' o' the Boyne."

"Still disnae make him a Scotsman," Annie said, smugly,

"Before he crossed that magic river it is reported that he swallied a dram o' Scotch and ate a good Scottish dinner – wi' his fingers." Andra said, pleased with himself for knowing history – besides Bowly McGeachie had told him that and if Bowly said it then it must be true.

"Don't tell me he had a fish supper?" Annie laughed, "And ate it wi' his fingers."

"He had mince and totties," Andra said.

Annie laughed loudly.

"Whit are you laughin' at?" Andra said. "Whit aboot that mafia godfather up there, where he shouldnae be, beside King William?"

"Whit aboot him?" Annie said suspiciously.

"He's a foreigner," Andra said.

"*That* is good Pope Pius the Tenth," Annie said.

"Tenth, twentieth, who cares – he's still foreigner," Andra said.

"But he is a *Saint*." Annie emphasised the word.

"So is His Majesty as faur as Ah'm concerned," Andra said.

"Tae become a saint," Annie began to explain, "ye must have performed at least two miracles. Whit miracle did Oor Wullie up there ever perform?"

"Sixteen-ninety, hen," Andra rubbed in the Boyne battle date with relish.

"Ye canny call that a miracle," Annie said.

"It is damn near it as faur as Ah'm concerned," Andra replied with a smile. "Ach, a' this has got nothin' tae dae wi' them next door. Ah mean when they come here they should at least have the courtesy for tae dress like us yins."

"Ye mean when in Rome . . ." Annie began.

"*Hey!*" Andra cried. "Away and wash yer mooth oot. That is wan word Ah will nut tolerate in this hoose."

"Ach, shut yer face," Annie sniped.

"Whit Ah'm sayin' is," Andra continued, "is that when in Glesca dae as we dae. That's a'. Ah mean oor lassies don't hide their faces – although, mind ye, some o' them should – and he should wear designer gear like whit ye can pick up at the Barras. He should take a tip frae me."

"*You?*" Annie laughed, "*You?* – designer claeths? Listen, ah see a wee man at the bus stoap every mornin' alang wi' his guide dug. He has a tailor's tape measure roon his neck making me think that he must be a tailor. When Ah see him Ah think aboot the claeths you wear."

"Ye think that wee man designs ma claeths?" Andra said.

"Ah think his dug designs your claeths," Annie said.

"Oh, ye dae, dae ye?" Andra said, hurt at his wife's attitude. He went on, "Don't you forget that time at Butlins when Ah won the top prize for ma appearance," he said proudly.

"Andra, that was a Wurzel Gummidge competition," Annie laughed.

"Well at least Ah don't go aboot wearin' a bed sheet like your pal Randy did," he said, screwing up his nose. "Ach, where did Ah go wrang. Whit did Ah ever dae tae the Big Yin up there tae deserve this? Ma whole life collapsin'. Banned frae the bus, thrown oot the ludge, bombed oot by the masons, ma idiot son away tae be a p . . . p . . . priest, ma lovely daughter married tae a wan fifty-five." Andra held his head in his hands and groaned.

"Wan fifty-five?" Annie said, puzzled.

"Aye, a fivety-two," Andra explained. "*And* oan toap o' that, ah've got the black an' white minstrels movin' in next door."

"Poor Andra!" Annie said sarcastically.

"Never you mind 'Poor Andra'," Andra said. "Ah have things in motion, so Ah have."

"Aye, you're full o' things in motion, Andra," Annie said.

"There's jist wan good thing in a' this," Andra said.

"Aboot whit?" Annie asked.

"Aboot them next door," Andra said.

"Whit's that, then?" Annie asked.

"They're no' Catholics – that's in their favour," Andra said.

"You just watch whit ye're sayin'," Annie said sharply, "Ah've said nothin' aboot you puttin' Oor Wullie up there oan the wa'. So just be careful."

"Ah've telt ye never tae refer tae His Majesty as Oor Wullie, Billy the Kid or anythin' else. Ah have said nothin' aboot your wee Ronnie Corbett staunin' there on the sideboard or Al Capone up oan the wa'," Andra retorted.

"Aye, well, you will refrain frae callin' St Francis 'wee Ronnie Corbett' and His Holiness, 'Al Capone'," Annie said sternly. "And another thing, Ah reiterate, Ah want you tae be oan yer best behaviour when oor Peter comes hame – ye hear me?" It wasn't a question. It was an order.

"Aye, well, just make sure ye put oot the lights when he comes in," Andra growled.

"Indeed Ah will not," Annie said angrily. "He is your son, tae, and you will gie him the respect he deserves."

"When is he comin'?" Andra asked hesitantly.

"Whenever he can get away," Annie said, happy at the thought. "He's comin' hame before he goes on tae the Scots College in Rome."

Andra blew a fuse. "Ah telt ye never tae mention that word in here never again," he cried.

"Rome – Rome – Rome —" Annie repeated, teasing her husband.

Andra clapped his hands over his ears and hurried into the bedroom. Annie laughed. She did love Andra and was used to his ways but at times could give him a good shake – and shake a lot of the stupid ideas out of him. She wondered what his latest ploy was? That uniform he had just received in the post what was that about?

CHAPTER FOUR

ANDRA HAD SLIPPED INTO HIS BLUE AND WHITE STRIPED PYJAMAS. His head hit the pillow. It had been a hard day. He was ready for sleep. He closed his eyes and fell into deep slumber, dreaming of the dream game.

Saturday arrived and the bus was already revving up outside McDougall's. Happy, singing fans were climbing on board ushered on by Sabastian. Wee Hughie was already on board occupying his favourite seat at the back – the seat he and Andra aways made a dive for – enjoying the singing which echoed up from the front. The large frame of Sabastian climbed on, he did a quick count and sat in the seat normally occupied by Andra. Hughie was not pleased. Sabastian would spot the half bottle of whisky hidden in the wee man's inside pocket. This was strictly forbidden. Sabastian was a stickler for sticking to the rules.

Andra arrived in time to see the bus turn the corner and begin its 189-mile journey to Manchester. His jaw fell although he knew Sabastian would not have allowed him on board anyway. He would miss the singing – the camaradarie – but he *would* see that game.

He turned away, head bowed, digging his hands deep into his pockets. But there was no jingle – no feel of copper or silver. In Andra's patois he was *skint*.

It would be hopeless asking Annie for a loan so that he could make his way down to Manchester to add his voice to the Old Trafford crowd. He wondered if he could sell the sideboard but soon discarded that idea. Annie would no doubt notice it missing from the living room.

Annie was nobody's fool and had even noticed that their bed was missing once when Andra sold it for a celebration after his team won a very important tie.Annie was not pleased and made him sleep in the bath.

Andra made his way to Central Station, pausing outside Oddbins, the Off-Licence shop, to get a whiff of their stock before going into the crowded station. He fumbled in his pockets and was delighted to find that he had enough loose change to buy a quarter bottle of whisky. He had heard of a ploy once on how to dodge paying the train fare and, as a last resort, had decided to try it. Nothing was going to keep him away from that game – even though he had no ticket.

Andra looked up at the departure board. The train would leave from Platform Two. He ambled along and was pleased to see the train already standing at the platform. Crowds were milling around with some obvious fans boarding the waiting train. Andra envied those happy supporters who were singing, waving their colours and enjoying themselves in anticipation of what was ahead.

He wandered along the station until he found a vacant seat right under the destination board, Andra sat down and contemplated his next move and wondered why the female on the tannoy system was talking in Swaheli? He stopped a man in uniform and asked what time the next train to Manchester was leaving. The man said that he was a Salvation Army officer and pointed up to the board. Andra looked up at the destination advice and panicked. The train would leave in five minutes.

He strolled down the platform, hands in pockets and whistling. He mingled with the travellers boarding and was soon seated in the warmth of a carriage which was rapidly filling up. He picked up a newspaper lying on the seat beside him and pulled it up close to his face. The guard's whistle blasted and Andra was jerked back as the train pulled out of the station. He was on his way. He wondered if he would meet up with Sabastian or wee Hughie? He would show them that he was independent. Yes, he would show them.

"Excuse me, please," a man's voice said. Andra shuffled closer to the window. His face was still buried in the newspaper but his eye *did* catch a glimpse of red as his fellow passenger slipped into the adjacent seat. The man *could* have sat opposite him at the other side of the dividing table, but hadn't. Andra wondered why. As though reading his thoughts, the man said,

"I like to sit in the direction that the train is travelling. I hope you don't mind?"

Andra shrugged. In fact, he thought, it was a good idea to have someone sit beside him. He wouldn't stand out like a sore thumb. He gave a sideways glance at his travelling companion. The red he had seen was the man's scarf, which was tightly wrapped around his neck. In bold letters were the words "Manchester United" – broken up but still understandable.

"Goin' tae the gemme?" Andra inquired.

The man nodded. "Wouldn't miss it," he said in a broad Lancashire accent.

"Me tae," Andra said, adding, "who dae you support?"

The man gave him a curious look. "Who do you think?" he said, pointing to his scarf.

"We wull gub youse," Andra said smugly.

"You think so?" the man said.

"Definitely!" Andra said confidently.

"What makes you so sure?" he said.

"We arra people," Andra replied, clicking his tongue against his cheek.

"What do think the score will be?"

"Twelve nothin' for us," Andra said with conviction.

"You are an optimist, eh?" The man smiled.

"Naw, Ah know nothin' aboot eyes," Andra said, "but oor new neighbour is wan o' them – he's lookin' for asylum."

The man brought his handkerchief across his forehead. "A bit warm in here," he commented, removing his scarf.

Andra's eyes leapt from their sockets. The man wore no necktie. And around his neck was the whitest dog collar Andra had ever seen.

"Ye . . . ye . . . ye're a minister?" Andra stammered.

"A priest," the man said. "I'm Father O'Brien."

The young priest offered his hand but the shock was too much for Andra. His eyes rolled and he slumped forward in a dead faint. Minutes later, although it seemed longer, he blinked his eyes open to find Father O'Brien giving him mouth-to mouth resuscitation. Andra yelled and jumped to his feet and vigorously drew the back of his hand across his mouth. His first thoughts were for a tetanus jag. He felt he was contaminated and now had leprosy.

He squeezed out and, seeing the rest of the carriage was fully occupied, slid into the seat at the opposite side of the table. It meant, of course, that he would now be looking straight at the priest. Andra put on his sunglasses. He felt that his retina would detatch, as it had with Peter, if he did not take precautions.

Trying to make conversation, Father O'Brien said, "You a Rangers fan?"

"Ah hiv been known for to grace Ibrox Park wi' ma presence," Andra said, a faraway look in his eyes. "For to gaze upon that hallowed ground," he went on, "where every blade of glass has been blessed by the Almighty. Where the sun ever shines on them eleven adonises, those gladiators with the magic skill wot has been bestowed upon their twinkling feet, whose trophy room rivals Fort Knox – that golden American bastion named efter another great Scotsman, John Knox. Aye, Ah suppose you *could* say that Ah am a Rangers supporter."

"Would you say you're devout?" the priest said.

"Ah am," Andra said. "Right now Ah'm devout any money."

Father O'Brien laughed. "Have you always supported the Rangers?" he asked.

"Ever since Ah was a boy," Andra said, proudly. "The first time Ah ever entered Ibrox and let ma eyes behold that garden of perfection Ah felt a glow come a' ower me, and every time since then when Ah enter Ah've always got a good glow on me."

Again, the priest laughed.

"Ma greatest wish is for tae be buried there," Andra said.

"Is it consecrated ground, then?" Father O'Brien asked.

"Naw, it's a' grass," Andra said.

Father O'Brien hid a smile, opened up his briefcase and produced a thermos flask.

"Coffee?" He said, pouring some into the silver cup.

Coffee?" Andra grimaced.

"You don't like coffee?" the priest said. "From Brazil," he added, "a good Catholic country."

Andra produced his quarter bottle and held it up. "Frae Scotland," he said, "a good Proddy country."

Andra took a long swig. He handed the bottle to the priest who accepted it reluctantly.

Father O'Brien took a despairing look at the ceiling, took a sip and coughed and got it over in a single gulp.

Andra hated himself for what he was doing but saw real

possibilities fraternising with the enemy. He urged the priest to have another sip.

"Get stuck in," he encouraged. "Sorry it's no' Vat 69, but ye'll need it for tae dull yer senses when ye witness the gubbin yer team wull be gettin'."

"So, where are your colours?" the priest asked. "You know - your scarf and that – how about your clappers?"

Andra pursed his lips. "That is a very personal question," he said. "It so happens Ah'm wearin' very tight y-fronts."

Father O'Brien smiled. The train thundered on on its way south. They talked and talked . . .

Andra felt very uncomfortable having to share his journey with the priest.

"Tell me, Andrew," Father O'Brien said.

"*Andra!*" Andra corrected.

"Yes – er – Andra tell me have you ever read the Good Book?"

"Ah don't believe in a lot o' it," Andra said.

"You don't believe in the Bible?" the priest said, narrowing his brow.

"Aw, ra Bible?," Andra cried, "Ah thought ye meant ma Dandy Annual. Ah jist don't believe that Desperate Dan can eat two cow pies at wance."

"No, I meant the Bible," the priest laughed. "It says we should all be brothers and love one another."

"How can Ah love the Pope," Andra grimaced. "Ah canny even understaun' how Ah'm sittin' here talkin' tae *you*."

"It's providence, Andrew – er – Andra, it's providence." Father O'Brien said, leaning over and patting his shoulder.

"Naw, Annie an' me are wi' the Co insurance. We are nut affilia . . . affil . . . er attached tae the Provi."

"You were saying your son is studying for the Priesthood?" the priest said, smiling.

"He is temporarily insane," Andra said.

"He is following his heart, Andra," Father O'Brien said.

"Aye, well he needs a transplant, "Andra said, adding, "Ah canny believe this, me sittin' here an' that back-tae-front coallar starin' right at me reminds me o' ma faither."

Father O'Brien's brows rose. "Your father was a clergyman? He wore his collar, as you say, back-to-front?"

"He wore his shirt back tae front," Andra said. "He was a very quiet and shy man. When ma maw met him he was walkin' backwards. An' at Barrowland, he always led when they were dancin'."

"Strange!" the priest said.

"He was an usher in the Arcadia picture hall," Andra said, "that's how he got intae the habit o' walkin' backwards. Even when they got married he walked doon the aisle backwards and ma maw had tae point him the right wey roon'."

Andra was feeling more uncomfortable as the train thundered on. He did not want to admit that he liked this young priest. Hughie and Sabastian must never know that he had travelled to Manchester in the company of a priest.

"Er – the Good Book," Andra began, "did it no' say somethin' aboot bein' good tae the poor?"

"Very much so," Father O'Brien agreed. "God loves the poor and down-trodden."

"Well he must really love me 'cos Ah am trodden rotten," Andra replied.

"Come, come," the priest said, "take courage."

"Whit dae ye think Ah'm daein'," Andra said, holding up his quarter bottle.

"I don't believe that you really don't like Catholics," the priest said.

"You'd better believe it, pal," Andra retorted.

"You married one, don't forget," Father O'Brien reminded him.

"How can Ah forget that?" Andra said. "Doon on her knees every night."

"Praying?" the priest said.

"Scrubbin'," Andra said. "Ah knew ma Annie was a scrubber the first time Ah laid eyes oan her."

"And, no doubt saying her prayers," the priest said, adding, "Don't forget that we're all Jock Tamson's bairns."

"How come, then, that we've got Rangers and Celtic supporters?" Andra argued. "If we were a' the same we'd a' be Rangers supporters – mind ye there widnae be as much fun."

"That's stupid," Father O'Brien said.

"Jist think aboot it," Andra said.

"How come you're travelling on your own?" the priest said, changing the subject. "Why are you not with your fellow supporters?"

"Ah missed the bus," Andra lied.

"Yes, I think you *have* missed the bus if you're so blinkered," Father O'Brien said, some sorrow in his voice.

"Listen you," Andra said, pointing a finger, "It's no' every Catholic Ah don't like. It's jist ninety-nine point nine per cent o' them. Ma Annie stinks o' caunle grease wi' a' her visits tae the chapel she keeps slidin' oot the bed. She's hung the Pope up oan oor wa' – unfortunately it's jist his picture right enough. Bein' a very tolerant person, Ah turn a blind eye. Ah even stick cotton wool in ma ears when she's prayin'."

"You can't get more tolerant than that," the priest agreed, hand to mouth hiding a smile.

"No' only that," Andra went on, "Ah never object tae her haudin' a prayer meetin' every Thursday night."

"A lot of Catholic women hold prayer meetings every week," Father O'Brien said.

"No' in the Royal Concert Hall they don't," Andra said.

Andra's eyes kept going to the carriage door. He was watching for the ticket inspector appearing. But no sign of him as yet.

"So, you're on your own, eh?" the priest said. "Missed the bus?"

"Aye," Andra said, allowing his mouth to droop.

"I had to meet a friend, a fellow priest," Father O'Brien said, "and we intended going with our party to Manchester. We are due at an ecclesiastical conference tomorrow and some of us football fans thought we would take advantage of our visit to take in the game."

"Aye, these Eccles . . . er . . . conferences can be dead borin'," Andra said. "A' that globe warmin' stuff an' that."

"Anyway, my friend couldn't make it – 'flu – and here I, too, am on my own. The rest of our party is in the next carriage with the Monsignor. I'm the 'overspill'.

"Shame!" Andra said without meaning. "Was yer pal a fitba' fan tae?"

"He was," Father O'Brien said.

"Then he'll no' need his ticket, wull he?"

"I suppose not," the priest said.

"Well, how aboot – er—?" Andra held out his hand.

Father O'Brien dug into his briefcase and produced the precious ticket. He handed it to Andra, whose eyes lit up.

"Ye widnae happen for tae have an extra rail ticket, would ye?" he asked hopefully.

"Afraid not," the priest said. "The Monsignor is holding all the tickets for our travel arrangements."

"*Whit?*" Andra cried. "Ye leave yer ticket wi' a Frenchman? Aw, that's jist askin' for trouble! The French canny be trusted, so they canny."

"Monsignor McGillicuddy is from County Cork," Father O'Brien said.

"That's worse," Andra said, "there's nothin' worse than an Irish Frenchman."

"The – er – ticket is for the Manchester end," the priest said.

"That disnae matter," Andra was jubilant, "Ra boys wull hear ma voice frae any end."

Father O'Brien was quite sure they would.

Andra, still feeling uneasy in the priest's presence, suddenly wished he had not wasted his whisky on this cleric. But, then, he *did* have ulterior motives right at the start, hoping to get the priest inebriated enough to part with his rail fare by fair means or otherwise. Still, he'd picked up a ticket for the "gemme" and that was just as important. His fare dodge plan could come into effect at the right time.

The priest was daft, he thought. If he had waved that ticket outside the Old Trafford gate he could have sold it for a few quid. Too bad about the train ticket tucked up in the Monsignor's wallet in the next carriage. Andra was happy that he had not gone into the other carriage packed with priests. He shivered at the thought. It was bad enough sitting here with just one of them – but a whole carriageful? He would have suffocated, he reckoned. *And* although he was in this carriage facing one priest, it would have been worse if he had been in there facing the Monsignor. Besides he couldn't speak French.

There had been no sign of a ticket collector during the journey. Maybe British Rail decided that with a trainful of priests there would be no fare dodgers. That, Andra thought, was to his advantage. His thoughts were interrupted by a strange voice.

"Time to go, John." Andra was startled. He looked up. The Monsignor was speaking English.

"Here already?" Father O'Brien said.

Andra looked out of the window at the large signpost which said "Piccadilly".

Father O'Brien rose, and shook Andra warmly by the hand. "I wish your team well," he said, "but I wish *my* team better."

Andra spat on his hand and vigorously rubbed it up and down his trouser leg. Contamination was a deadly thing and he was taking no chances. With that, Father O'Brien left the train. Andra looked out of the window. For a moment he thought he was back in Rome. A whole sea of white collars were chattering down the platform. He shuddered.

He sat down and watched the train empty. The passengers headed down the platform to the barrier where two uniformed men stood and checked tickets. Andra took a large swig of what was left of his quarter bottle. His breath would be just right. He alighted from the train and stood swaying and waving his bottle on the now empty platform.

"We Arra People," he sang with gusto.

"Hey you." The voice came from the uniformed gentleman running up the platform towards him.

"You talkin' tae me?" Andra slurred.

"Yeah, you," the man said. "What are you doing here?"

"Ish thish the Glesca train?" Andra hiccupped.

"It is," the man said.

"Good." Andra said and went to board.

"Hey, wait a minute," the man cried, hauling him back by the shoulders. "Where do you think you're goin'?"

"Ah am goin' back tae the greatest country in the world," Andra said and burst into a chorus of *I Belong To Glasgow*.

"Not on that train, you're not," the man said.

"You said that was the Glesca train," Andra protested.

"It is," the man said. "It's the train that's just *arrived* from Glasgow. The train *going* to Glasgow leaves from Platform Three – just over there." He pointed towards the platform.

"Right," Andra said, snapping his heels and saluting smartly before staggering off.

"Just a minute," the official said. "Show me your ticket for Glasgow."

"Hivnae got wan," Andra said.

"I thought as much," the man said. "Right, c'mon you," he added and, taking Andra by the arm, led him down the platform to the barrier.

"You'll get a ticket over there," he said, nodding towards the ticket office. And, with that, he shoved him through the gate.

Andra joined a crowd heading for the street exit. Once outside he brushed himself down and was directed to Old Trafford by a friendly policeman. His jaw dropped as he neared the ground and saw the Rangers' supporters' buses pass him. He could hear the raucous, cheery singing and felt the joy spilling out. What had he done to deserve this? To be ostracised from the club and the bus was like having a contagious disease. Something like being a Celtic supporter at the Rangers' end at Ibrox.

But he'd be back, yes, he'd be back. Andra was sure of that. The Rangers team would complain. Andra's voice was needed. He could hear the team now.

"Where is Andra?" would be the cry from the worried players as they ran down the tunnel to the roar of the crowd.

*   *   *

The game proved to be an unspectacular one with no scoring at the final whistle. Andra left the ground, his chin scraping the pavement. A nothing-nothing draw was not worth his trouble coming down all this way.

Not only had he defrauded British Rail but he had to suffer the indignity of sitting with a priest all the way down. He wondered if he would come out in a rash? Maybe little red blotches – all resembling the Pope's face – would break out all over his body. Andra shuddered and put the picture out of his mind. Now, how to get back to Glasgow? That was the immediate problem. He dare not use the same ruse again. Besides, to Andra's mind, the railway boys at Glasgow's Central Station were more astute than their English counterparts. No way would they fall for that trick.

Andra sighed as he saw the Rangers supporters' bus flash past him with their vibrant voices still singing – although he wondered what they had to sing about. They should have cuffed

73

Manchester. That referee was wearing double-glazed specs, he decided. Ach, it was a waste of time.

"Andra . . . Hey, Andra . . ."

Andra turned. Hughie Broon was hurrying through the crowd towards him. Breathless, Hughie grabbed Andra's elbow.

"Andra, how did you get here?" he panted.

"Don't ask me, Hughie, don't ask me," Andra said, pulling his arm away. "And staun back, Hughie," he added. "Ah do nut want for you tae get constipated."

"Whit dae ye mean?" Hughie asked, puzzled.

"That haun o' mine came – by mistake – intae contact wi' a p . . . p . . . priest," Andra shuddered.

"Aw, ye mean contaminated," Hughie said.

"Aye, that as well," Andra agreed. "Look at me, Hughie," he said. "Am Ah a' oot in blotches, is ma coupon a' full o' wee red pictures o' the Pope's face?"

Hughie examined Andra's face closely. "Naw, just yer normal plooky skin, Andra, nae faces oan it."

"Thank God for that," Andra said, wiping his brow. "Ah was sittin' next tae a priest oan the train and Ah thought Ah might've got constapa . . . er . . . whit you said."

"That's daft," Hughie said. "Sure ye don't get contaminated frae Annie."

"Naw, but Ah'm immune tae Annie," Andra said. "She's like a vaccination."

Hughie laughed. "So, how are ye gettin' hame?" he asked.

"Ah don't know yet," Andra said.

"Well, c'mon," Hughie said, taking his arm, "Ah'll have a word wi' Sabastian. He might hate ye but Ah canny see him lettin' a fellow supporter doon."

Andra beamed and slapped Hughie on the back. "Thanks, ma wee pal," he said.

Sabastian was already standing by the bus and ushering the boys on. He looked up as Hughie and Andra approached.

"Whit's this then?" he glowered.

"Andra made his ain wey doon, Sabastian," Hughie explained, "but he's got nae wey o' gettin' hame."

"In that case he can stey here and good riddance tae him," Sebastian snapped.

"He *is* wan o' the boys, Sabastian," Hughie pleaded, "an' he *did* come doon here for tae support them. We canny jist abandon him here, so we canny."

"Until we have a meetin' of ra boys for to discuss Andra Thomson's attitude, he is nut welcome aboard oor vehicle." Sabastian said gruffly. "He has brought no' only oor local club intae disrepute but Rangers fans everywhere."

"Ah've done nothin' for youse tae take that attidude," Andra said, almost crying.

"Find yer ain wey hame," Sabastian said, pushing Hughie on board and stepping on himself before slamming the door shut. The singing immediately started on the crowded bus and Andra watched sadly as it roared into life and sped away. He could hear the echo of the boisterous tunes as it vanished round the corner.

Hughie had wrapped his Rangers scarf around his pal's neck hoping it might soften Sabastian's attitude when he saw Andra. Andra walked on following the street signs. It was getting colder now and he was thankful for Hughie's scarf. He tied it more tightly and, head bowed, walked on.

He didn't hear the screech of tyres pull up alongside him. But the voice made him look up.

"Hey, pal, want a lift?"

Seeing the scarf, a supporters' bus had pulled up.

"Miss yer bus, china?" the fan called.

"Er – aye – aye, that's right," Andra replied, grateful for that eagle-eyed fellow supporter who had seen him on the road, the long, lonely road.

Seconds later he was on board the warm, cosy bus and joining in the singing. Somebody thrust a can of beer into his grateful hands and the raucous bus headed north towards Glasgow.

Andra stepped off at George Square after wishing everybody a happy new year – although it was the middle of April – and hoping for a better result next time.

He made his way across the square, down Glassford Street and into Trongate where he caught a number nine tram going up London Road and on to Auchenshuggle.

CHAPTER FIVE

ANNIE, FEATHER DUSTER IN HAND, TURNED AS ANDRA ENTERED. She gave Pope Pius a final flick and, eyeing Andra, said flatly, "And where have you been?"

"It's a long story," Andra said, "and seein' you're busy, Ah'll no' go intae that the noo. Ah see ye're gien' Al Capone the beauty treatment, and don't forget His Majesty up there."

"Ah will not lift a finger for Oor Wullie or his cuddy," Annie snapped.

"That's no' nice tae call that magnificent hoarse a 'cuddy'." Andra said, "and less o' the Oor Wullie."

"Andra," Annie began, "Ah'd have mair respect for oor Wullie, there, if you wurnae so thrawn, so unbending. Ye've got tae live and let live Andra, tae respect other peoples' point of vew. Tae be less bigoted."

"Whit dae Ah dae that makes ye think Ah am bigoted?" Andra was genuinely hurt.

"Well," Annie began, "there's wee things like ye suddenly develop a spit when we pass the chapel. How ye refuse for tae eat rice when Ah put it doon tae ye – sayin' you wull have nothin' tae dae wi' anythin' that comes oot o' a *paddy* field. How ye used tae make me walk a' the wey tae Rutherglen when we went tae the Rio just because ye widnae go oan a green caur – wee things like that, Andra."

Andra shuffled his feet and gazed at the floor. "Och Annie," he said, putting his arm around her shoulder, "that's jist me. Ah don't mean any herm. It's the wey Ah was brought up. Like faither, like son, as they say. And don't anybody ever say ma faither was no' a great man." Andra puffed out his chest.

"Ah canny argue," Annie said, "Ah never met him."

"Aye, he *wis* a great man," Andra repeated. "Like me he played the big drum in the walk *and* he was a special constable."

"Whit was so special aboot him?" Annie asked.

"He was only three-feet two," Andra replied. "When he played the drum in the walk a' you could see was the drum walkin' doon the street."

"Was he as bigoted as you?" Annie asked.

"Ah keep tellin' ye Ah'm no' bigoted or racist. Ah don't care whit anybody is just as long as they're white and a Proddy. Everybody's got me wrang."

Annie saw no point on going on with the conversation. Changing the subject, she said, "Ye jist missed Jean an' wee Hymie."

"*Hymie!*" Andra threw up his arms. "Ma grandson – *Hymie,*" he groaned. "How could oor Jean gie her wean a name like that – wee *Hymie?*"

"Because he's a good Jewish boy," Annie said. "Don't forget oor daughter is married tae a fine Jewish lad – an architect." Annie was proud of Jean and her choice of husband.

"Whit was she thinkin' aboot?" Andra moaned. "There was plenty o' her ain kind goin' aboot."

"And whit's her ain kind?" Annie said stiffly.

"Well, there's wee Malky, the midgie man for a start. An' then there's Davie McPherson, who's faither is a heid bummer in the Masons."

"Aye, we know why you wanted Jean tae get pally wi' him, don't we?"

Andra, ignoring the remark, retorted, "Whit an ugly wean Wee Hymie is, tae. Whit a hooter he's got oan him. Pinocchio's got nothin' oan him. But that's a trait wi' that race, intit?" he said, screwing up his own sizeable "hooter".

"That is rubbish," Annie snapped. "Jist like sayin' a' Scotsmen are mean or Irishmen are thick. It's just a load o' rubbish. Wee Hymie's nose isnae any bigger than yours."

"Naw?" Andra said. "Well, Ah was oot wi' oor Jean wan day and she was pushin' wee Hymie alang the Clyde Walkway when Wee Hymie sneezed."

Whit aboot it?" Annie demanded.

"The *Ark Royal* answered," Andra said.

"Rubbish," Annie said. "And, even if it did whit's that got tae dae wi' anythin'?"

"The *Ark Royal* was anchored in Rothesay," Andra said.

"Ye're talkin' a load o' twaddle, as usual Andra," Annie said angrily. "It's aboot time ye grew up and came doon tae earth. A' they places ye've been slung oot of – does that no' tell ye somethin'?"

"Aye, it tells me they're a' daft. But, as General McArthur said, 'Ah wull return'."

"Aye, but will ye chinge? – that is the question," Annie said.

"Aye, if it pleases you, hen," Andra said.

"Nae mair spittin' as ye pass the chapel?"

"Ah'll suck a *Locket* sweetie," Andra said.

"Nae mair refusin' tae eat yer rice?"

"Ah'll even eat it wi' chopsticks," he said, "when Ah've got ma chops in, that is." Andra laughed

"Aye, well, we'll see," Annie said.

The musical doorbell rang out with the strains of *The Sash*. Andra immediately jumped to attention and saluted.

"Ah'll get it," Annie said. She returned moments later with Wullie.

"We've nae sugar tae spare," Andra snapped, remembering Randy's daily request for a cupful.

"Oh, I'm not wanting sugar," Wullie said. "I thought that you, being a typical Glasgow-onian, could help me with some of your customs so that I could pass them on to Saddam who is doing a Glasgow project at school."

Andra's chest puffed out ten inches. He was delighted that Wullie had recognised his knowledge of *his* fair city. "Aye, nae bother," he said. "An' the first thing ye'll need for to learn is that we are *nut* Glasgow-onians. We are Glas-wegians – like the Norwegians."

"Right," said Wullie.

"Aye, right," Annie said, "Ah'll jist get oan wi' ma housework and leave you two to it." She disappeared into the bedroom.

Andra and Wullie sat facing each other. Andra pulled his chair closer.

"Glasgow," Wullie began.

"Glesca," Andra corrected.

"Er – yes, Glesca," Wullie repeated. "I'm told it means the 'Beautiful Green Place?'"

"Who telt ye that?" Andra snapped. "It means the Beautiful *Blue* place."

"Right," Wullie said and repeated, "the Beautiful *Blue* Place."

"Noo," Andra said, "the first word ye must learn if ye want for to be a true Glaswegian is the 'F' word – right?"

Wullie nodded and Andra grabbed him by the cheeks and pressed them together, "Noo, say it," he commanded, "Say Fi – Fi –"

Wullie struggled to follow Andra's example, his cheeks being compressed by Andra's strong fingers. "Fi . . . Fi . . ."

"That's it," Andra said, "ye're getting' it. Fi . . . Fi . . . Fit . . . Fit . . . keep goin'."

"Fit . . . Fit . . ." Wullie struggled.

"Good!" Andra said, slapping him on the shoulder, "noo, keep goin' Fit . . . Fit . . . Fit-*Baw*. Fit-*Baw* – get it? *FITBA*'!"

Wullie repeated the word perfectly.

"Noo," Andra went on, "say R . . . Ri . . ."

Wullie was getting the hang of it. "Ri . . . Ri . . .' he repeated.

"That's it," Andra said, "Rain . . . Rain . . ."

"Rain . . . Rain . . ." Wullie smiled.

"Good!" Andra said.

"You talk about your weather, eh?" Wullie said.

"Naw, naw, nothin' tae dae wi' the weather," Andra said, "Rain . . . Rain . . . for *Rain-gers* . . . Rangers . . . get it?"

"Got it," Wullie said.

"Good!" Andra said.

"What is Rangers?" Wullie asked innocently.

"*Whit is Rangers?*" Andra cried, repeating, "*Whit is Rangers?* Whit dae ye mean, '*Whit is Rangers*' ?"

"Yes, I ask," Wullie said.

"*Whit is Rangers?*" Andra was beside himself.

"I'm new," Wullie said.

"An' if ye ask a question like that ye'll no' get aulder, son," Andra said. "Rangers is the greatest fitba' team in the world, that's a'." Andra was shocked that anybody on this planet did not know of *his* team.

Annie, who had been listening at the bedroom door, just in case of 'accidents', shouted. "They got beat twelve-nothin' last week."

Andra immediately jumped up, dashed across the room and banged the door shut. "Listen Wullie," he began, "if ye want tae

79

be a citizen of this country there are things ye need tae know."

"Like what?" Wullie asked.

"Like who won the European Cup Winners Cup against Moscow Dynamo, in Barcelona, in 1972. That was wan o' the great moments in Glesca history."

"Who won it?" Wullie asked.

"Are ye daft?" Andra bawled. "Who else but ra boys, that's who. If ye want for tae be a citizen ye must know aw these things."

"Anything else I should know about Gla – er Glesca?" Wullie asked.

"Definitely," Andra said. "For instance did ye know that Rock n' Roll was invented by a wee Glesca boy frae the Gallygate. His name was Elvis McPresley – some nuts erroneously called him Ra King – but this is nut true. There is only wan king and that's him up there oan that wa'. Noo claeths," Andra went on, "Ye must get the right Glesca gear and the first item ye must buy is a bunnet. Ye must walk aroon like we dae – or, *if* you are goin' tae an Auld Firm match, buy a steel helmet."

Wullie nodded.

"Noo, you wull have tae chinge yer eatin' habits," Andra went on. "Nae mair camel stakes. Tae be a true Glaswegian ye must eat fish n' chips or mince and totties and don't forget the Setturday night must."

"What's that?" Wullie asked, puzzled.

"It's the Glesca sign of good neighbourliness," Andra said. "Ye must buy a boattle o' Bells whisky, pour yersel' wan good dram and sit doon and listen tae the Alexander Brothers oan the wireless, then go next door tae yer nearest neighbour – that's me – and gie him the rest o' yer boattle."

"But I am a Muslim," Wullie protested. "We do not drink alcohol."

"Aw, whit a shame!" Andra said. "In that case ye don't take a good dram oot yer boattle – ye haund in the boattle intact – us bein' Christians up this close, we are allowed for tae drink anythin'. Dae ye believe in Jesus?" Andra asked.

"We follow Mohammed," Wullie said.

"Wee Mohammed who owns the coarner shoap?" Andra said with incredulity.

"No, no," Wullie said, shaking his head. "Mohammed, the great prophet."

"Aye, that's who Ah mean," Andra said. "Wee Mohammed doon the road. He's makin' a great profit in that wee coarner shoap o' his."

"*Andra!*" Annie bawled. "Wullie is talkin' aboot a different Mohammed, don't show yer ignorance."

"Jesus, too, was a great prophet," Wullie said.

"Ah, but he didnae own a wee coarner shoap," Andra said. He looked up only to be met by Annie's glowering eyes. He coughed and changed the subject.

"Are ye intae fitba'?" he asked.

"My two sons, Saddam and Osama are Partick Thistle supporters," Wullie said.

"They are definitely no' right in the heid. Ah canny see them amountin' tae much," Andra said.

"Osama is hoping to get a trial with Thistle while we are here in Gla – er Glesca," Wullie said.

"It's you that should be tried," Andra said. "Keepin' joabs aff us joab-seekin' citizens."

Annie let out a loud, rasping laugh. "Joab-seekin' citizens? There's a laugh," she said. "The last joab *you* went efter was a government appointment – and there's another laugh."

Wullie was impressed. "A government appointment, eh?" he said.

"Ye had as much chance o' gettin' it as Ah have o' bein' made Betty Grable's understudy."

"Zat's so?" Andra sniped. "You've got a better chance o' bein' King Kong's understudy."

"Ye only went efter it because ye got a uniform wi' it and ye thought it would be a piece o' cake."

"You didnae want me for tae get it because you're a Catholic," Andra said.

"Rubbish!" Annie said. "You knew fine ye widnae get it but because ye went efter a joab and didnae get it, it cleared ye wi' the broo and yer money would continue," Annie retorted, "and, another thing, ye liked the idea o' wearin' a uniform."

"There's nothin' wrang wi' that," Andra said. "Uniforms can be smart – as you will soon be seein' for yersel'."

"What *was* this wonderful joab with a uniform that you did not get?" Wullie asked.

"He applied for the joab of Archbishop of Canterbury," Annie said, throwing her eyes towards heaven.

Wullie laughed.

"It proves that Ah'm religious," Andra said.

"Your wife says you are a bigot, Mr Thomson," Wullie said. "Is that true?"

"It's a lie," Andra said. "Ah jist don't cross masel' when Ah pass the chapel. Ah cross the road. Ah happened for tae be of a different religious persuasion, that's a'."

"That's fair enough," Wullie said. Then, to Annie, he said, "Well, Mrs Thomson, that seems fair. Aren't you glad to see your husband coming in and standing up for his faith?"

"Ah'm jist gled tae see him comin' in and staunin' up, period." Annie said.

Wullie laughed and Andra frowned.

"I believe your son is about to become a priest?" Wullie said.

"He is not the full shullin'," Andra replied.

"You must be honoured," Wullie said.

"Ah should've got the V.C. right enough," Andra said. "For the time Ah crawled oot tae no-man's land and cerried back a wounded officer."

"That was very brave," Wullie said."And why didn't you?"

"He was a German officer," Andra said. He shook his head as he remembered.

Andra wondered why he was sitting talking to this foreigner. Not only talking to him but giving him advice. He did not want Wullie thinking that he had been accepted and was welcome to the *Beautiful Blue Place*. Obviously mental illness ran in Wullie's family if his son, Osama, hoped to play for Partick Thistle. In Andra's mind this ambition showed that the boy was definitely an imbecile.

"It *is* wonderful to be here in this *Beautiful Green Place*."

"*Blue Place*," Andra corrected.

"Er – yes – the *Blue* place. I have a heart complaint and I hope to get a heart transplant here," Wullie smiled.

"*See!*" Andra cried, pointing a finger at Wullie. "They are just here for tae take a' they can get frae us for *nuthin'*."

"What's it to you?" Annie said.

"Plenty," Andra snapped. "We have oor ain folk waitin' for transplants. Hearts are hard tae come by ye know. Folk don't want tae jist gie them away tae foreigners." Turning to Wullie, he went on. "It's a wonder you didnae have a heart attack when wee daft Osama said he wanted tae play for Partick Thistle."

"I felt my heart jump with pride," Wullie said.

"Aye, well Ah've a good mind tae plant wan oan ye masel'," Andra said angrily, "a *fist* transplant!"

Taking Wullie by the arm, Andra steered him towards the door. "Away you in tae yer ain hoose, take wee daft Osama in yer erms, cuddle him and throw him oot the windae." With one shove Wullie was on the landing as the door slammed behind him. Andra stepped back into the room where Annie stood with arms folded and a grim look on her face.

"That was a terrible thing tae say tae that poor man, tellin' him tae throw his wean oot the windae," she said angrily.

"Well, the boy's obviously no' right in the heid," Andra said.

"You've a cheek," Annie retorted. "The wee boy is just daft oan fitba' – you're just daft, period."

"Well, he should be back in the jungle kicking somebody's heid aboot."

"Andra, you get right in there an apologise tae that poor man," Annie snapped, pointing at the door.

"*Apologise!*" Andra cried. "Ye widnae get me goin' intae that den of a hundred curries. They'd probably stick me in the pot."

"So, whit's new?" Annie said. "Ye're stewed every Setturday."

"Killin' just rolls aff their back," Andra said. "In the jungle it's a wey of life. They're used tae it. They see some poor missionary, their lips smack and their mooths watter, so, oot comes the knife and that's that – dinner is served."

"Ach, away ye go!" Annie snapped. "It would need a real sharp knife tae cut *your* throat – ye've got a real brass neck."

Andra ignored his wife's rant. He flopped on to an easy chair and Annie retired to the kitchen leaving him to his thoughts. Wait until she saw him in his new regalia, his uniform from the American brotherhood of the Freemasons, he thought. He would show them. Yes, he would show all of them.

⋆　⋆　⋆

Andra slept soundly that night although the ghostly Dalbeth voices chanted *twelve-nothing* for at least half-an-hour after his head hit the pillow.

Annie, as usual, was up first in the morning and Andra's *All Bran* was already, as usual, waiting for him on the kitchen table.

"Sleep well?" she asked as he entered, scratching his head.

"They bloody voices kept me wakened for a while," he moaned. "Ye'd think they'd have better things tae dae than try and keep a man aff his sleep – they're supposed tae be deid."

Annie went to the door when she heard the letter box flap. The postman was early, she thought.

"It's for you," she said, handing Andra the letter.

Excited, he tore it open. After a quick perusal he thumped it down on the table with a cry.

"Noo we'll see!" he cried.

"Whi . . . whit is it?" Annie stammered.

"They're sending wan o' their top men up tae see me," Andra guffed, delighted.

"Who is?" Annie asked.

"The Masons." Andra said proudly. "They have decided for tae vet me wance again."

"When is he comin' up?" Annie wanted to make sure the house was tidy.

"They didnae say. It'll be a surprise visit. It's definitely unusual but they said it was because Ah am unusual."

"They're dead right there," Annie agreed.

Andra was beside himself with joy. He marched over to *that* picture, snapped his heels and saluted smartly. "This must be *your* doin', Your Majesty and Ah thank you frae the boattom o' ma untransplanted heart. Ah wull nut let you down and, if ye were here right now, Ah would shake ye by the hand – in the proper secret fashion."

The musical sound of *Immaculate Mary* echoed through the house.

Andra let out yell, ran over to the sideboard drawer, took out some cotton wool and plugged his ears. "Ah am getting' that chinged," he wailed.

"Andra, that was the deal," Annie reminded him. "Your song and ma song, remember?"

Andra regretted the day he ever agreed to the deal. He hated when Annie's liturgy group met in his hoose for their weekly meeting. Eight or nine of them all arriving at different times making the doorbell sound like a cathedral service.

Annie hurried to the door and entered with Hughie.

Andra, mouth full, nodded.

"Ah had tae tell ye, Andra, that there's a meetin' o' Sabastian and the boys this moarnin' for to discuss your request o' gettin' reinstated," he said.

Andra jumped up and clapped his hands. "Oh Boy!" he exclaimed. "This is definitely ma lucky day."

"How, hiv ye won the coupon or somethin'?" Hughie asked.

"Better than that, Hughie," Andra said, slapping him on the back, "better than that," he repeated. "Ah must put on a clean shirt," he said, hurrying into the bedroom.

"He must really be excited," Hughie said, "Puttin' oan a clean shirt, eh?"

"Even just puttin' oan a shirt's an improvement," Annie said.

"Ah hope they vote him in again," Hughie said.

"Aye, we might get some peace then," Annie replied.

Once again the doorbell blasted out *Immaculate Mary*.

"This place is like Central Station this moarnin'," Annie said, hurrying to the door.

Hughie was startled by a sudden scream of delight from the lobby.

A beaming Annie entered, hanging on to her son Peter's arm. Peter wore the clerical collar and a dark suit.

Hughie warmly shook Peter's hand.

"Oh whit a lovely surprise!" Annie said, squeezing his arm. "Ye look just like a priest."

"We're allowed to wear the collar," Peter said.

"Ye look like Bing Crosby in *The Bells of St Mary's*," Hughie said.

"Don't tell me you went to see that picture Hughie?" Peter said, surprised.

Hughie shrugged. "Naw, Ah didnae," he said, "Ah picketed the Olympia when it was in it, cairryin' a placard protestin' alang wi' yer da', sayin' 'Never mind the Bell's o' St Mary's, visit the Come Inn Pub, in Stevenson Street, and get the *real* Bells – in a boattle and seventy proof – but Ah saw Bing's photay outside."

Peter laughed. "Aw, Hughie," he said, "you hivnae changed."

"And neither has yer faither," Annie said.

"Ye mean he still isn't used to living here in the high flats overlooking Celtic Park?" Peter asked.

Annie shook her head. "Remember he used tae chuck chuckies ower the windae at the Park? Well, Ah'm no' gonny tell ye whit he chucks ower noo," she said, despair in her voice.

"Bad as that, eh?" Peter shook his head. What was he going to do with this father of his?

"The aulder he gets, the worse he gets," Annie said, "even his ain folk want nothin' tae dae wi' 'im. He's been thrown oot o' the Rangers Supporters' Club, the Orange Ludge. The Masons and the Brigton Croass Communist Party want nothin' tae dae wi' him."

"Where's the man himsel'?" Peter asked.

"He's in there puttin' oan a clean shirt," Annie said, nodding towards the bedroom.

"How's Jean and Clarence and wee Hymie?" Peter asked.

"Aw. Just wonderful, Peter," Annie beamed. "They've got a lovely hoose in Newton Mearns – but yer faither still canny accept that Jean married outside her faith. He didnae hauf gi me a showin' up at their Jewish weddin' last year."

"Oh, how?" Peter asked.

"He started gien daft Masonic signs – as he thought – tae Clarence's auld grandfaither when we were sittiin' at the table. And he thought the auld man was gien them back tae him. He was that pleased he got up, ran roon the table tae see the auld man, stuck oot his tongue and put his fingers in his ears and started wagglin' them and gave the auld man the shake o' the haun – wi' his erm stuck roon his back."

"Embarrassin' right enough," Peter said.

"Everybody was lookin' at him." Annie went on. "Especially as it turned oot that auld man had nothin' tae dae wi' the Masons. He's got St Vitus Dance. But, here, you come and sit doon and Ah'll make ye a cuppa tea."

"Thanks Mum," Peter said.

Annie vanished into the kitchen.

Peter turned to Hughie. "Well, Hughie," he inquired, "and how are you?"

"Tae tell ye the truth, Peter," Hughie said with furrowed brows, "Ah'm worried aboot yer faither. He was telt tae haun' his drum in yesterday but it had acne but that's no' the reason for his expul . . . erexpolution."

"Ah've never seen a drum wi' acne," Peter said, hiding a smile.

"Oh. Aye, oan its skin," Hughie said.

Andra, smiling broadly, came into the room. The smile vanished the minute he saw Peter there. Quickly, he turned on his heel and vanished again.

"Hey Andra," Hughie innocently called out. "Look who's here."

Andra re-entered the room wearing a black "sleep mask". He fumbled about like a blind man, bumping into furniture and feeling his way around. "Ma retina has been detached," he moaned.

"It's yer boy, Andra," Hughie said.

"He's nae boy o' mine," Andra snapped, and, going over to the picture on the wall, put his hand over King Billy's eyes. "Hide yer royal eyes, Your Majesty," he said, "and this is nut a sight for yer faithful cuddy either."

"Och, Dad, you're still not on about this," Peter pleaded.

Andra did not look at him. "Ah see yer maw's got Gunga Din up there next tae His Majesty," Andra stated. "Ah know it was a deal we made but Ah was afflicated by some mad sympton at the time. Ah had the same trouble that you hiv – temporarily insanity. And as for you," he turned on Hughie, "wan word o' a' this tae anybody and you wull be attending the Eye Infirmary."

"Ah'm yer pal Andra," Hughie said, hurt.

"Only while ye're still livin', Hughie," Andra said and, turning to *the* picture, "Your Majesty," he said, "Ah am sorry that you have had for tae witness this indignity, especially hivin' tae hing up there next tae that auld mafia boss. But Ah sweer tae you on John Knox's grave that it'll no' be for long. You are about for to see a new me."

Annie came in carrying a tray with a pot of tea, two cups and a plate of Abernethy biscuits. Placing it on the table she cried, "Hurrah! Ye mean we're getting' rid o' the auld you? Nae mair drum practice at midnight, nae mair bawlin' oot the windae and saying yer tunin' up yer voice for Ibrox?"

Andra scowled. "Less o' the sarcasm," he said. "And, as for you," he said to Peter, "is it no' aboot time you were getting' back tae yer cemetery?"

"You mean Seminary, Dad," Peter corrected.

"Ah know whit Ah mean," Andra said.

"He's been talkin' tae that hoarse again," Annie said.

"Ah do nut talk tae the hoarse," Andra cried, "although Ah'd get mair pleasure oot o' that than you get talkin' tae Gunga Din there."

"Don't you dare call His Holiness Gunga Din," Annie cried. "He disnae like hingin' up there next to Oor Wullie any mair than Ah like it."

"Noo, Ah've telt ye before, His Majesty is nut tae be referred tae as Oor Wullie," Andra said angrily.

"Never mind Dad, there's a good time coming," Peter said, slapping Andra on the back.

"You've been readin' the *Beano* again," Andra replied.

"Tell me, how did ye like Rome?" Peter asked, winking at his mother.

"Ah'd rather have a foartnight in Hell," Andra grimaced. "The place stinks o' garlic."

"Did you see the Holy Father?" Peter asked.

"Wullie Waddell widnae be seen deid there," Andra said.

"And what about the catacombs" Peter asked.

"Ah hate cats," Andra said.

"Oh, it was wonderful!" Annie said, clasping her hands together, "His Holiness came oot oan tae the balcony and waved doon tae us. Ah just pictured it was you up there, son, wan o' these days."

"Don't you dare become the Pope," Andra snarled.

Hughie nodded. He agreed with Andra.

"Dead right Andra," he said. "You would definitely be barred frae the ludge – no' tae mention the bus."

The thought was too much to contemplate. Andra shook his head. "Ma life would definitely be ruined," he wailed. "Can ye just imagine it – me goin' intae McDougall's. 'Whit's yer lassie daein' these days,' wan o' the boys asks? 'Oh, she's a teacher in a

Jewish school,' Ah say. 'And yer boy?', he asks. 'Oh. He's the Pope,' Ah say."

"Aw, ye'd definitely get barred, Andra," Hughie said.

"Ah'd definitely get murdered, Hughie," Andra said.

Annie's mind was still in Rome. "It was just a dream," she said, with a faraway look.

"Just a bloody nightmare," Andra said.

"It made me proud o' ma faith when Ah saw him up there, like a faither lookin' efter his flock," she said dreamily.

"That's how Ah feel as well," Peter said.

Andra drew him a scornful look. "You hivnae got feelins'," he said.

"How can ye say that tae yer ain son?" Annie snapped.

"He's nae son o' mine." Andra said bitterly. "The minute he put oan that collar he strangled me."

"Ah didnae know ye were deid, Andra," Hughie said.

"You shut up ya wee idiot or you'll be deid," Andra snapped.

"Stop this nonsense," Annie sniped. "Peter is whit he wants tae be an' that's it."

"Ah wanted him tae be a plumber," Andra complained.

"Peter got the call," Annie said, squeezing her son's arm.

"Had ye left the windae open, Peter?" Hughie said.

"Whit makes ye say that?" Peter drew down his brows.

"Well, yer maw says ye got the cauld," Hughie said. "Mind ye when ye canny button up and wear a tie it's no' healthy."

"Ah don't think that's what she meant, Hughie," Peter smiled.

"Ah meant Peter's got a vocation, Hughie," Annie explained.

"Oh, where did ye go, Peter?" Hughie asked.

"He got a call from God, Hughie," Annie said.

"Aw, that was nice!" Hughie said. "It would be long distance, eh?"

"Ah heard His voice in ma heart, Hughie," Peter said, pointing to his chest.

"Whit did he say?" Hughie was all ears.

"He said, 'Take the cloth, my son, take the cloth," Peter said.

"And you thought he was tellin' you for tae be a priest?" Hughie was interested.

"Of course," Peter said.

"Maybe he wanted you tae be a tailor," Hughie said.

"Ah always knew Peter would be a priest," Annie said. "Ah was haudin' ma rosary beads when he was delivered and he grabbed them oot ma haun. Ah knew then that there was somethin' different aboot him."

"That he was daft?" Andra said.

"Ma maw was haudin' a boattle o' Johnny Walker when ma brother Erchie was delivered and he grabbed it oot her haun," Hughie said.

"Don't tell me he became a publican?" Annie said.

"Naw, a drunk," Hughie said.

Peter decided to steer the conversation away. "So, Mum," he began, "you're well and truly settled intae your 27th floor high flat, eh?"

"Oh. Aye, Peter," Annie said smiling. "A bit noisy right enough when the O'Reillys were next door and a bit smelly wi' Randolph walkin aboot wi' his smelly stick and chantin' a' day. But things should be quieter noo that we've got a nice black gentleman steyin' next door and Randolph's deid."

There was a sudden racket from Wullie's house as African drums began to beat loudly, followed by hysterical screams. Everybody stuck fingers in their ears.

"Geez! Whit's goin' oan? It's voodoo time!" Andra cried.

A loud, urgent rapping at the door had Annie hurrying, in a panic, to answer it.

Holding his heart, Wullie rushed in, and flopped on to the couch.

"Whit is it? Whit is it?" Annie asked, fear in her voice.

"He's probably ate somethin' that didnae agree wi' him," Andra said cynically. "Probably wan o' the weans."

"The – the – the *GHOST*!" Wullie gasped. "Walking and chanting."

"Was it Randy?" Andra asked.

"I don't know how it was feeling sexually," Wullie said.

"Naw, a meant – it sounds like Randy – was it wearin' an orange sheet?" Andra asked.

"A white sheet," Wullie said, "it was wearing a white sheet."

"Just as long as it wisnae a green an' white sheet," Andra said.

"Calm doon Wullie," Annie said, patting his head. "It's been yer imagination."

"It was no imagination," Wullie said. "I saw it. I tried the old African drum trick to get rid of it but it only made it chant louder."

"Drums can dae that," Andra said. "Ah remember oan wan walk an' Ah was marchin' doon Dalmarnock road bangin' ma drum, wimmen were hingin' oot their windaes and it's amazin' whit came oot o' they windaes."

"Chants?" Wullie asked.

"Chantys, some filled," Andra said.

"Well, that ghost gave me a turn," Wullie said, holding his chest.

"Whit kinda turn?" Hughie asked. "Singin', dancing?"

"Maybe Ah can help?" Peter said.

Wullie's hopes rose. "Oh, could you?" he cried. "I can see you're a man of the cloth, please help – perhaps you could exorcise it."

"Ah don't know if press-ups an' dumb bells are gonny be any good," Hughie said.

"You are the only dumb bell aroon here, ya wee clown," Andra sniped. Peter and Wullie exited the room and left for next door.

"Are you frightened o' ghosts, Annie?" Hughie asked.

"Hughie, Ah've been livin' wi' spirits for years," Annie said, giving Andra a knowing look. The suggestion was lost on the wee man.

"Did yer ghost chant?"

"*Chant!*" Annie cried, "A' the time Hughie: 'Ra boys – Ra boys'. "

It suddenly dawned on Hughie what Annie meant. "Aw," he cried. "Aye, right enough, Andra gets cerried way."

"He has been, oaften, Hughie," Annie said," but he keeps comin' back."

A racket erupted from Wullie's house. Annie's hand came up to her mouth. "Oh, Ah hope Peter's a'right," she said worriedly.

"If he hisnae been cooked by this time," Andra said sarcastically.

"You be quiet!" Annie snapped. The noise got louder and Annie got more worried.

"That ghost must be hauf wi' tae hell by noo," Hughie said.

"Don't be so sure, Hughie," Annie said. "Spirits and rotten

smells are hard ta get rid o'. Ah know by experience."

"Ah think Sabu's got his pet elephant in there and that's no' allowed. Pets are no' allowed in these hooses. It's a council rule – nae cats or dugs allowed. An elephant's got nae chance." Andra was adamant.

"Ye're dead right, Andra," Hughie said. "Ah had tae hide ma crocodile."

"Quite right," Andra said.

"Ah think it must be Randy," Annie said, after thinking things out.

"Geez! That's a' Ah need. Just back hame efter two weeks o' hell and whit dae Ah find? Ah find Ah'm livin' next door tae Al Jolson who's got a Randy elephant in the hoose."

"Ach, away ye go ya racist midden," Annie retorted. "There's nae randy elephant next door – come tae think of it, it's been years since there's been anythin' randy aroon here."

Everything fell silent and Peter returned.

"Where's Wullie?" Annie asked.

"He's exhausted and is lyin' down," Peter said.

"Whit aboot his elephant?" Andra asked.

"Elephant?" Peter was puzzled.

"Never mind yer daft faither," Annie said, "Whit aboot the ghost? Did ye get rid o' it, son?"

Peter shrugged. "Ah canny be sure," he said. "Ah saw it walk through the wall."

"That disnae mean anythin'," Andra said. "These wa's are dead thin.Ah could spit peas through them, so Ah could. It's embarrassin' just how thin they are. Ah can hear whit that big blonde, Bella whit's er'name and her man Ebeneezer get up tae in bed."

"They'll no' hear anythin' comin' frae your bed, that's for sure," Annie said sarcastically.

"Zat that big stoater wi' the St Bernard dug?" Hughie asked, smacking his lips.

"Aye, that's her and 'cos you hear whit's goin' on in her bed disnae mean the wa's are thin," Annie said.

"Annie," Andra snapped. "She lives in the close."

"Ach, shut up," Annie said. "Let's see that parcel ye're bein' so secretive aboot."

"No' possible, Annie. That's the point – it's a' aboot secretiveness."

Annie raised her eyes towards the ceiling. "Ye're in yer ain hoose – we've nae secrets here. Ah'll no' tell anybody." She put her finger to her lips.

"Ah have been accepted intae the Mason's chapter in America," Andra said proudly. "And that is ma regalia wot they have sent. Ah admit it looks a bit unusual but, then, it *is* a secret society and ye don't want for tae advertise that you ur a member."

"A'right, then," Annie said, "ye've made yer point, let's see ye in it?"

"Naw, naw," Andra said, "Ye'll have tae wait till the time's right."

"And when will that be?" Annie asked curiously.

"You'll see," Andra replied.

"How did ye have tae apply tae America, Andra?" Hughie was puzzled.

"Hughie," Andra said. "Sometimes ye have tae leave yer ain country for tae be recognised."

"Ah'd recognise ye anywhere, Andra," Hughie said.

"Ah mean for yer genius tae be recognised, Hughie," Andra explained.

"Are you a genius Andra?" Hughie asked, impressed.

"Ah shine sometimes, Hughie," Andra said.

"On a Setturday night he's usually got a good glow," Annie said.

"Whit dae ye mean by that?" Andra said, annoyed.

"Andra," Annie said, " Ah saw ye gie a wee man a light the other night."

"So, whit's wrang wi' that?" Andra said.

"Aff yer nose, Andra," Annie scoffed.

Hughie was impressed. "Noo, that definitely is genius," he said, admiringly.

"Ach, it was nothin'," Andra said shyly.

"Ach, c'mon, Andra," Annie piped up. "Let us intae the secret."

Andra thought it over. After all Annie *was* family, he decided and Hughie *was* his best pal, daft and all that he was. Andra cleared his throat.

"Well, a'right," he said. "Seein' the Masons in Brigton rejected ma application for to join them, Ah decided for to apply tae wan o' the branches in America, Brazil tae be exact. Ah saw saw their advert in a magazine. Send a subscription and you're guaranteed for to be accepted. Full gear will be supplied. A' Ah had tae dae was send them a cheque for ten pounds, made payable to MM – that means Mason Membership – and that's it. Well ma gear came but Ah hivnae tried it oan yet. Ah'm too excited."

Annie was doubtful, She was sure Andra was telling the truth but the whole thing sounded like a scam to her. "Well, Ah' don't know, Andra," she said sceptically, "Ah'm suspicious so Ah am. The Freemasons don't advertise for members – efter a' they're a secret society."

"Aye, well, just ta make sure," Andra said, "Ah have re-applied tae the Brigton branch. Noo that Ah'm a brother o' the American branch, it might cairry some weight and Ah'll expect they will consider me."

"So we'll need tae wait before we see ye a' dressed up in yer splendour?" Annie said.

"Aye, Ah'll show them, " Andra said with determination.

"Whit are ye gonny show them, Andra?" Hughie asked, curiously.

"Never you mind, Hughie," Andra said.

Peter was beginning to feel sorry for his dad. He knew he was a racist and a bigot and was way over the top. But he *was* his father and Peter went by the Good Book – "Judge not that ye be not Judged".

The doorbell rang out with *The Sash* and Annie hurried to answer. She entered with Wullie, who was holding his head. Wullie made straight for Peter. "I can't thank you enough, Father," he said.

"He's no' a father yet," Andra corrected.

"Well, father or not, he got rid of that ghost," Wullie said.

Annie had been thinking hard. Turning to Andra, she snapped, "Where did *you* get a ten pound cheque tae send tae America?"

"Ah selt the dug and bought a postal order," Andra said, pleased with himself.

"We hivnae got a dug," Annie said.

"That's because Ah selt it," Andra said.

"We've never had a dug, Andra," Annie snapped.

"Well. Ah selt somebody's dug," Andra argued.

"Was it a Jack Russell?" Hughie asked.

"Ah didnae know the dug's name," Andra said.

"There's nae dugs up this buildin' except for Big Bella's St Bernard in the close. And she knows full well that it's no' allowed," Annie said.

"Well, I just came in to thank the reverend gentleman for his assistance," Wullie said, leaving the room.

"My pleasure," Peter said.

"And Ah'll away an' lie doon," Andra said.

"And Ah'll away an' tidy up," Annie said, heading for the kitchen.

Peter and Hughie flopped on to the couch.

"A wee bit advice, Peter," Hughie said.

"Oh, aye, whit's that, Hughie?"

"Ah widnae get too friendly wi' Wullie if Ah was you," Hughie said, seriously.

"Why no'?" Peter asked, wondering what Hughie was on about.

"He's a cannon Ball," Hughie said.

"Oh, aye, and who told you that?" Peter said, hiding a smile.

"Yer faither," Hughie said.

"Oh, yes, and Dad's always right, isn't he?" Peter said facetiously.

"And Wullie loves tae eat holy people," Hughie added. "Yer faither says he liked nothin' better than a missionary in the pot wi' an ingin' thrown in as well."

Hughie was definitely influenced by Andra and Peter decided to put him in the picture.

"Look Hughie," he said, "Ma Dad's no' always right. You shouldnae let him influence ye. He's a racist and a bigot but, Ah think, underneath it all he's no' such a bad bloke."

"He's a rare drummer," Hughie said, "And Ah know for a fact that he disnae like the Pope – me, tae."

"Well, Ah don't know whit oor Holy Father has done tae you," Peter said. "Is it this Pope in particular you don't like?"

"Naw, we don't even like the deid wans as well," Hughie said proudly.

Peter could only laugh. He rose. "Well, I'd better be getting' along, Hughie," he said, heading for the door. "Now don't you go wanderin' next door, hear me? Or ye might just land up on a plate."

"Ah'll just sit here and think aboot your poor faither's awful pickle – oot the supporter' club, oot the ludge. Nae masons or nuthin'," Hughie commiserated. "Ah just want tae sit here and constipate for a while."

Peter laughed and left.

CHAPTER SIX

PETER STROLLED DOWN DALMARNOCK ROAD. HE PULLED UP HIS coat collar as the fine drizzle hit his face. He was thinking of Andra and despite everything, he felt sorry for him. Maybe a word with the Almighty might help? Passing the Sacred Heart chapel he noticed the main door was open. This was unusual as thieves and vandals had no fear of God. Obviously workmen had been in repairing something or other – *all* churches had their own something or other that needed repairing. His thoughts were confirmed when he noticed a couple of buckets of plaster in the porch. He saw no-one as he entered. The workmen were obviously taking their tea break – as is their wont or maybe pub break in the nearby hostelry. Peter walked down the centre aisle to the echo of his own footsteps. Votive candles flickered, throwing shadows against the stone walls. He slid into a pew near the altar, bowed his head and prayed.

"Lord," he began, "I'm here about my father please hear me. He is going through hell, if you will pardon the expression. His whole life is falling down about him and he is very unhappy. Rangers getting beaten twelve nothing last week has only added to his misery. He's been banned from their club, banned from your Orange Lodge, the Freemasons – in fact everything he holds dear in this life has been taken from him. He makes Mum's life a misery. Please help him and I promise never again to mention Celtic in my prayers but – let them skelp Aberdeen this Saturday – and thanks."

Peter felt better now that he had passed on his burden to "higher authority".

*　*　*

Annie, out shopping, popped in to pay a visit when she noticed the door open. Seeing Peter kneeling down near the front, she quietly joined him. "Hello, son!"

"Ah, Mum," Peter said, a little surprised. "Ah felt Ah just had to have a word wi' God on ma father's behalf."

97

"Ah think God's forgotten yer faither," Annie said sadly.

"Ah think that it's Dad who has forgotten *Him*," Peter said. "He's forgotten how to pray."

"Naw, naw," Annie said, "Ah hear him in bed every night, lyin' there next tae me – prayin' a' the time. He thinks Ah'm sleepin' – and Ah might as well be. He prays, Ah'm tellin' ye. 'Oh Lord, put dynamite in Rangers' boots – let them massacre Celtic every time they meet. On a Friday make every fish in Glesca poisonous and gie us eighty-two degrees o' glorious sunshine next Tuesday when we haud the walk – and Ah promise tae pey double for ma *Rangers News* every week'. He's talkin' aboot gettin' it printed and haunded oot ootside the Central Station."

"He does take things a bit far, doesn't he?" Peter said. He had been brought up with his father' prejudices but, as a boy, they didn't mean anything to him. Only as he got older did he realise how stupid it all was. He saw how his mother's faith strengthened her and fell into it himself *and* it grew stronger until he felt he wanted to devote his life to the church. He had many friends, too, on the "other side" – many of them Orangemen and members of his father's lodge – but without his hardened bigotry.

Peter wondered if the Almighty heard his prayer. And, more importantly, if he did, would he answer it?

"Yer faither's just fitba' daft son," Annie said, defending Andra, "Ah should've known the day o' oor weddin'. He came doon the aisle wearin' a blue and white tiled hat and scarf and twirling his rickety."

"Where is Dad?" Peter asked.

"He's lyin' doon," Annie said.

"Is he tired?"

"Naw, he's drunk," Annie said, adding, "Ah'd better dash. The man frae the Masons telephoned tae say he was comin' up tae see yer faither." Annie pecked Peter's cheek and hurried out.

"Maybe the Almighty *has* heard my prayers," Peter thought.

Not to show ingratitude, Peter closed his eyes, clasped his hands together and prayed. "Lord," he said, "many thanks for this sign. I pray that all will go well with my dad and that he will find some peace." Peter knelt in silence until an authoritative voice boomed and made him jump.

"Peter, my son," the Heavenly voice said, "I have heard your prayers, your pleas have reached me. Do not worry about your father – Andrew – er Andra will find the peace you seek – the yoke will be lifted from his shoulder – and don't put any bets on Celtic this Saturday."

Peter, scared out of his wits, got up, genuflected and hurried from the chapel – stopping only to make a quick sign of the cross at the holy water font on his way out.

★   ★   ★

McDougall's pub was packed when Wee Hughie walked in. Sabastian was standing on a table in the corner and a sea of blue and white scarves surrounded him.

"Noo, quiet please, boys," he was saying, "order, order."

"Hauf and a hauf pint," one wag piped up.

"No' that kinda order, less o' the kiddin'," Sabastian snapped. "We a' know why we ur here. We are here for tae hear the appeal o' former colleague Andra Thoamson who has asked for tae be re-instated to oor ranks – wi' a' the privileges that entails – goin' oan the bus an' that. His advocate hisnae arrived and so we wull continue without him."

"Andra Thoamson disnae drink advocat," a wee man said.

"Aye, a'right," Sabastian said, "Ah see we've got the comedians here wi' us."

"Ah *AM* here," Hughie Broon called, forcing his way to the front.

"Ah, Hughie – come in, get up here," Sabastian said.

Hughie climbed on to a chair and with Sabastian's assistance, clambered on to the table.

"Noo you ur here on Andra Thoamson's behalf, that right?" Sabastian said.

"Ah am," Hughie agreed. He cleared his throat and began. "Andra is just back frae his hoaliday and disnae know that Ah am here speakin' on his behalf. Noo, Andra has been chucked oot of oor club because the chairman here thinks that he's too bigoted and brings us intae disrepute – as some of youse think as well. But he isnae. He is just over enthusiastic – right enough he disnae like Catholics and blacks an' that, but he's as true blue as you or me." Hughie was getting into his stride.

"Where was he oan hoaliday?" somebody shouted.

Hughie ignored this. "Andra is a true Proddy," he went on, "and has never wance said a hail Mary except for the time when he was lyin' in the Royal at death's door efter drinkin a boattle of Parazone he thought was vodka. *And* the only reason he uttered that prayer was that he wanted wan o' *them* tae snuff it and no' wan o' us. But he survived despite his urine sample meltin' the test tube. The cat lapped it up and was last seen screamin' oot the door wi' its hair staunin' straight up never tae be seen again. Tae show ye how loyal he is, he was gonny throw himsel' oot the windae when he heard whit had happened tae the cat – especially when he heard it was an orange cat. He still refuses tae eat his greens because o' their colour."

"So, where was he on holiday?" the voice piped up once again.

"Whit does it matter where he was on hoaliday?" Hughie answered, annoyed at the interruption.

"Ah'd've asked him for tae bring me back a stock o' rock," the voice from the crowd said. Everybody laughed.

"Noo, less o' the frivolity," Sebastian ordered. "We are here oan some serious business. Noo, Andra Thoamson has asked for tae be re-admitted tae oor ranks, go on, Hughie."

Once more Hughie cleared his throat. "Ah've been a pal o' Andra's ever since Ah first met him in the barber's when we baith went in for a shave. Ah was quite surprised tae see him sittin' there, talkin' tae the barber aboot worldy affairs while gettin' a close shave."

"How was that?" a voice enquired.

"He was only eight at the time," Hughie said. "Jist goes tae show ye how long Ah've known him."

A murmur buzzed round the gathering. Sabastian interrupted.

"It's true he gets us a bad name and Ah hate him anyway. But if we could prove he was an idiot then we would be exonerated."

Hughie shook his head. "Ah don't think he is," he said. "But Wee Senga, president o' the Brigton Croass Communist Party thinks he is.When she asked him whit he thought o' Karl Marx he said be preferred Groucho."

"Whit a stupit thing tae say, "the voice from the crowd said. "Anybody knows it should be Harpo." A titter went round the crowd.

"It is widely assumed," Hughie went on, pleased that he had remembered the word *assumed* where he'd heard it in a Spencer Tracy picture, "that Andra is a heavy drinker and will drink anythin'. That is not true. He'll no' drink Guinness or Crème de Menthe."

"How's that?" Sabastian asked.

"Well, Guinness speaks for itsel' and Crème de Menthe's colour puts him aff." There was a round of applause.

"We'll have nane o' that," Sabastian cried.

"He likes a Blue Lagoon," Hughie said. This was greeted by another round of applause.

"Well, Ah just don't know," Sabastian said. "He does take things a bit too faur – he is over the top. Ah mean Ah was in the library, in Landressy Street, wan day when he came in and asked the lassie for a book called *How Blue Was My Valley* – noo, that's goin' a bit too faur, so it is." Everybody laughed.

"And," Sabastian went on, "Ah believe that he wanted for tae emigrate tae Kentucky when he heard that it was the Blue Grass State. Ah do nut know if that is true."

"It's a lie,"Hughie said. "He wants to be buried at Ibrox Park and will not leave Glesca in anticipation o' that fateful day. The only stipul . . . er stipu . . . stripantorium is that they fly the Ibrox flags at hauf mast when the time comes." A murmur of approval went round the crowd.

"Well, be that as it may," Sabastian said. "Ah believe that we have here today a member of the Orange Ludge who is interested in the fate of Andra Thoamson."

"Dead right," a wee man in the crowd piped up and gave his big drum two loud bangs to announce his presence.

"Would ye staun up please," Sabastian called.

"Ah am staunin' up," the wee man said.

"Right, go ahead," Sabastian said.

"Andra Thoamson," he began, "is the best big drum banger we hiv ever had. But, he does go ower the tap. The last time we were oot walkin' Ah noticed that he had plastered a picture o' the Pope on his drum and was gien it laldy. *That* is against the rules and Ah made him remove it."

"Quite right!" Sabastian said. "It gies us a bad image. Ah must admit, though, he had some voice. He encouraged the boys at

Ibrox wi' his voice – the whole crowd could hear him."

"Imagine that – the whole o' Ibrox could hear him!"

"The whole o' Parkheid could hear 'im," Sabastian added.

"For a while we thought he might just be unbalanced," the wee man said.

"Aw, naw, he walks fine – just when he's drunk he might be a wee bit aff balance," Hughie said, sticking up for his pal.

"Naw, naw," the wee man said, "that's a different thing. We thought he might be an idiot."

"So did Ah," Sabastian said. "Whit made *you* think that, wee man?"

"Ah noticed, oan wan o' oor walks, that he was wearin' a Celtic jersey. Noo, you jist don't wear a Celtic jersey oan an orange walk," the wee man said.

"Whit was his explanation?" Sabastian asked.

"He said he thought it would get up the noses o' the Catholics we passed."

"That makes sense," Sabastian said. "So he canny be an idiot." Once more a murmur of approval went round the crowd.

"Ah think we should hiv a vote," Sabastian said.

"Well, we *dae* need a big drummer," the wee man said. "And he *is* wan o' the best. If he would just tone doon a bit."

"Right," Sabastian said. "Hauns up those who say he can come back?" The majority put up their hands.

"Right," Sabastian said, "Ah'll go up and see him."

"Me, tae," the wee man said, giving his drum a loud bang.

"Where was he on hoaliday?" the same voice cried.

"Hughie?" Sabastian said, looking at Andra's china.

"Well – er aye – er – he was in – er – Rome."

All hell broke loose in the pub. There were cries of protest and the wee man could not control his right arm as it repeatedly banged his drum.

"*QUIET – QUIET!* everybody," Sabastian's voice hollered. Silence fell.

"Rome, eh?" Sabastian said, quizzically. "Noo, that is not cognizant wi' the spirit of this Rangers Supporters Club."

"*Or* as a member o' the ludge," the wee man said.

"Ah wull go up and see him," Sabastian said.

"*See who?*" Andra's voice boomed as he entered the pub.

"We were voting to see if you should be allowed back intae the club," Sabastian said.

"*And* the ludge," the wee man added.

Andra strolled over to the wee man and took the drum from him. He gave it a few loud thumps, blew on the drumsticks, turned and said, "*AND?*"

"We canny decide if you're an idiot or no'," Sabastian said.

"Ah tried ta tell them you're no'," Hughie butted in.

"You *dae* gie us a' a bad name," Sabastian said.

"Ah didnae always hate Catholics," Andra said. "It a' started wan day years an' years ago as Ah was passin' a chapel oan ma wey hame wi a poke o' wulks. When suddenly this man came flyin' oot the chapel and mugged me. Gave me a right tankin' for nothin'."

"Maybe he didnae like wulks," Hughie said.

"Ah knew right away it was a Catholic that did it," Andra said.

"How did ye know?" Sabastian asked.

"It was the priest," Andra said.

"And that made ye bitter?" Sabastian asked.

"There's naebody mair bitterer than me," Andra said.

"Ye're that bitter that ye went oan a hoaliday tae Rome?" the wee man said sarcastically.

"Ah was hopin' that Ah could talk the Pope intae joinin' oor ludge," Andra said seriously, "an' Ah'm sure oor eyes met when he came oot oan his wee ledge. He shouted somethin' tae me but Ah couldnae understaun' it."

"How? Was it in English?" the wee man said facetiously.

"Ah think it was in Italian or somethin'," Andra said. "Anywey, the bloke staunin' next tae me translated it."

"Whit was the Pope sayin'?" the wee man asked.

"He said. 'Twelve Nothin'," Andra replied. "Ah didnae know whit he meant."

"A wee bird telt me that your son is away for tae be a priest, zat true?" the wee man asked. The entire crowd leaned forward,

"A stool pigeon, was it?"

"True, is it?" the wee man asked.

"Ma son is temporarily insane," Andra replied.

"He was seen goin' intae a chip shoap wearin' a brown Franciscan habit," the wee man said.

"That is *nut* a habit," Andra said adamantly. "That is his nightgoon."

"He was seen, at night, goin' intae the chip shoap wearin' his nightgoon?" the wee man said in disbelief.

"He sleepwalks," Andra said coldly.

"Another thing," the wee man said, "your wife was seen goin' intae the chapel. Whit ye say aboot that?" The wee man screwed up his eyebrows.

"Annie went in tae blaw the caunles oot and stick oot her tongue," Andra explained.

"Ah don't believe ye," the wee man said.

"Ur you callin' me a liar?" Andra said, clenching his fists.

"Why did yer nose just grow two inches there?" the wee man said.

"It's runnin'," Andra said.

"Wull you two chuck it?" Sabastian said, stepping in between them.

"You shut up," the wee man said.

"Aye, you shut yer geggie," Andra said.

"Aw, wait a minute," Sabastian said. "Ah'm the wan that called this meetin' tae see if we're gonny take you back?"

"Aye, well he's no' getting' re-instated in ma ludge till Ah'm sure this Catholic connection isnae true," the wee man was just as adamant. "He'll have tae prove tae me that he's a' there and is faithful to oor cause," he added.

"Listen," Andra said. "His Majesty hings oan ma wa' and every night Ah staun before him and salute him. At Christmas Ah lay a bunch o' flooers under his picture – orange lilies, for to be exact. And for his faithful hoarse, Orange Rum, descendant of the great communist hoarse, Red Rum, Ah lay a bowl o' Scotts Porage Oats. It's the only hoarse in Scotland that can throw the caber."

"Ah think you are no' the full shullin'," the wee man said, "and Ah wull not allow ye back intae ma ludge until ye prove that ye are not affiliated tae them Catholics."

"Ah've stoapped goin' tae see Bing Crosby pictures," Andra said.

"That disnae count," the wee man said.

"You are no' fit for tae be in the ludge yersel," Andra said, angrily. "Look at ye – ye're the spittin' image o' Barry Fitzgerald."

"And you're a dead ringer for ma wife – and Ah canny staun her either," the wee man said.

"Ach, shut yer face," Andra snapped, "the time wull come when you are beggin' me tae come back tae the ludge and you," he said, turning to Sabastian, "wull want tae hear ma voice at Ibrox. Ah'm tellin' ye!"

"Ach, shut yer face," the wee man said.

"Aye, well, you can keep yer bloody drum," Andra said. "It's the only drum Ah've seen wi' acne oan its skin."

"Listen you," the wee man said, drawing himself up to his full five-foot two height, "just watch it. The day *you* get back intae the ludge Ah'll join the Knights of St Columba."

"*And*," Andra retorted, "if you ur still the heid bummer in that lodge this time next year, no' only wull ma son become a priest *AH'LL* become a priest." Andra gave the drum two loud bangs and pushed it towards the wee man.

"You beat it," he snapped and stormed out, followed by Hughie.

$$\star \quad \star \quad \star$$

Andra tossed and turned that night. He kept thinking of the wee man and his uncompromising attitude. He did not like the comparison between himself and the wee man's wife. He had seen the wife once when on a visit to Calderpark Zoo. She had been standing looking into the chimpanzee compound, causing Andra to run to the head keeper's office shouting that one of the chimps had escaped. He had only made matters worse by offering her one of his bananas. But he would win in the end, he was sure of that. He awoke with Annie shaking him vigorously.

"Andra – Andra!" she cried. "Andra, get up!" He never knew he could leap from bed so quickly.

"Whit is it? Whit is it?" he cried excitedly.

"Ye're gettin' a visitor," Annie said as Andra struggled into his trousers.

"Geez! Ah thought the hoose was on fire – or worse still, Ibrox was on fire," he cried.

"Put on somethin' decent," Annie ordered.

"How, who's comin' – the Queen?" Andra said with sarcasm.

"Naw, no' the queen," Annie said, "a Doctor Somebody."

"Ah don't need a doactor," Andra snapped, beginning to remove his trousers and hop back into bed.

"Well, don't collapse when Ah tell ye that it's somebody frae the Masons that's comin' up this mornin' tae see ye – a Doctor Somebody – he jist phoned."

Andra let out cry of delight. "Yahoo! Whit did Ah tell ye?"

"Aye, well, ye'd better get yer skates oan as well as yer troosers," Annie said. "He didnae say whit time he was arrivin'."

"That's their wey," Andra said knowingly, "Try and catch ye oot."

"Ah wonder why they're sendin' a doactor up?" Annie said, puzzled.

"Because, ye see, the Masons is full o' intell . . . er intellect . . . er brainy folks – like doactors. Lawyers and even traffic wardens." Andra was pleased to show his knowledge of the Freemason system.

"Mmm!" was all Annie could say.

"Here, Ah'd better get ma new American uniform on," Andra said, snapping his fingers. "Jist tae show that Ah have been accepted intae the American branch and this is jist a formality."

"Aye, ye better dae that," Annie said, casting a glance at the ceiling.

She brought out the duster and began a systematic dusting all around the room. Standing before the pictures of King Billy and Pope Pius, she hesitated, meticulously dusted down the Pope and gave the King a quick flick.

Andra had retreated to the bedroom to make himself ready for his very important visitor.

The telephone rang, making Annie jump. "Hello," she answered, "Aye, he's in – right. Ah'll tell him." Annie hung up.

"Andra," she called, "somebody called Sabastian is comin' up tae see ye."

"Right," Andra called from the bedroom.

The phone had hardly settled in its cradle when it shatterd into life once more. Annie sighed. Who could this be? She answered. "Aye, he's in – right, Ah'll tell him."

"Andra!" She called once more.

"Whit is it?" Andra called, impatiently.

"Somebody called 'the wee man' is comin' up ta see ye."

"Aye, right," Andra called.

The sound of *The Sash* rang out from the doorbell. Annie answered and entered the room with a tall, distinguished gentleman.

"I'm Doctor 654, from the branch of you-know-what," he said.

Annie curtsied. "Andra is just getting prepared for to meet youse," Annie said in her in best Kelvinside *patois*.

"I'm here as a branch vet," the doctor said.

"Oh, we do not have a dug," Annie replied. "They are nut allowed in our hooses by the council."

"No, I am here to vet your husband for membership," the doctor said.

"Are you a real doctor or is that an horrible degree given out by your organisation?" Annie asked.

"I am a psychiatrist," the doctor said. "I have to vet that your husband is not mentally disturbed – have you ever found him so?"

"He does get a wee bit disturbed if Rangers lose," Annie said. "I remember wance he threw a bottle of mulk oot the window."

"What's so disturbing about that?" the doctor asked.

"The Catholic mulkman was still haudin' it," Annie said.

"I just want to make sure he is not unbalanced," the doctor said. "Have you ever found him so?"

"Only on a Setturday night coming back from McDougall's have I seen him unbalanced," Annie said.

"McDougall's?"

"Yes, it's the local hostile. It's where the fans meet after a gemme to discuss the tactics of the match – a kind of Post mort – post depression, if you like," Annie said.

The doctor smiled and strolled over to the wall pictures. "Ah!" he said. "King William. Eh?"

Annie grimaced and the doctor noticed. "Andra just adores that picture," Annie said.

"Do you think your husband loves the king more than he does you, that it?" he said.

"Ah think he loves the hoarse mair then he does me," Annie said.

Immaculate Mary from the doorbell rang out. Startled, Annie hurried to answer and entered with Sabastian who was carrying an important-looking piece of parchment.

"Whit song was that?" he asked, puzzled and nodding towards the door.

"It's called *Rangers Forever*, composed by Father O'Donnell of the Benedictine Monks," Annie lied.

"Oh!" Sabastian nodded, "Is he in – Andra – is he in?"

"He's jist makin' himsel' decent," Annie said.

"Ah've got some good news for him," Sabastian said. "This is a certificate re-instatin' him intae the club – providing Ah can prove that he is of sound mind and is no' an idiot as the high heid yins think, and wull never bring the club intae disrepute ever again."

Once more *The Sash* rang out and, sighing, Annie answered. She came back with a smiling Hughie Broon.

"Er – this is Andra's pal, Hughie Broon," she said, introducing him. "Hughie, this is Doctor 123 of the Freemasons."

"Er – Doctor 654," the psychiatrist corrected.

"Whoops, sorry," Annie said. "Ah was never any good at numbers."

Hughie was in awe. He stuck out his tongue, stuck his thumbs in his ears and waggled them before going into a soft-shoe shuffle.

"Who is this, Fred Astaire?" the doctor asked.

Hughie followed up by asking the one important question Bowly McGeachie had taught Andra and himself to greet a brother. "Has your granny got a wart on her bum?" he said.

"Not a mark," the doctor said, catching on to Hughie's thinking.

Annie interrupted. "Hughie is Andra's best pal," she said.

"We ur related through drink," Hughie said proudly.

"Whit's keepin' Andra?" Sabastian said. "Ah telt ma wee boy Ah was goin' oot tae buy him wan o' the 'Gers new strips. Ah left him lyin' oan the flair wailin' an hammerin' it wi' his fists."

"Whit's he wailin' for?" Annie asked.

"He's a Celtic supporter," Sabastian said mournfully.

"Ur you here for tae take Andra back intae the fold?" Hughie asked cheerily.

"Wance Ah can say that Andra is a' there – then he is back," Sabastian said.

Hughie was delighted. He had visions of them both being at the back of the bus singing lustily. Of visits to McDougall's together, drinking merrily and enjoying great football conversation.

Sabastian was getting more impatient, He stood up and went over to the wall pictures .

"Ah see good King William here," he said. "But is that no' the Pope next tae him?"

"That is ma faither," Annie said.

"Is he goin' tae a fancy dress ball?" Sabastian asked. "Ah do nut believe that man is your faither," he added angrily.

"He is everybody's faither," Annie said proudly.

"He's no' ma faither," Hughie said. "Ma Da' was cock-eyed."

Once more the doorbell invaded the house with its musical tones. "It's becomin' like Central Station in here," Annie grumbled as she hurried to answer.

Annie returned with the wee man, who was carrying the big drum. He gave it a good wallop and sat down with the instrument between his legs.

"Andra in?" he said curtly.

"He's getting' ready," Annie said, wondering what was keeping her husband.

The wee man cleared his throat. "Er – Ah have come here on the instructions of higher authority for tae haund this big drum back tae Andra. Ah must gie him the benefit o' the doubt that he is nut an imbicile Ah'm telt – although, personally, Ah think he is an idiot. Still, we ur a democratic organisation and Ah must dae whit Ah'm telt frae the high heid yins."

Hughie began to applaud but Annie wondered where all this would lead to. Andra was bad enough but when he saw that they were all running after him he'd become hard to live with. Not forgetting the midnight drum-practice.

The doorbell rang out once more, Annie tutted and hurried to answer it, returning with Peter in his Franciscan habit. Stunned, everybody jumped up. The wee man whipped out a pair of sunglasses and put them on while Sabastian closed his eyes tightly and stumbled round the room. Doctor 654 yawned and glanced at his watch.

"Who is this?" the wee man snapped.

"This fine young priest-to-be is *my* son and, believe me, Andra wisnae thinkin' oan how fortunate he would turn oot when he was conceived."

"Does Andra know aboot *him*?" Sabastian asked.

"Of course he knows," Annie snapped.

"He never let on," he grumbled.

"And why should he?" Annie said angrily. "How come yer ain wee boy is a Celtic supporter?"

"He got kicked in the heid by a Guinness hoarse and has never been the same since," Sabastian said despairingly.

A cry came from the bedroom.

"Ur youse ready?" Andra hollered.

"Come oot for heaven sake, " Annie replied. We're a' waitin'."

Andra leapt out – three feet in the air and shouted – "*VOILA!*"

All stood stock still. Doctor 654's mouth fell open as did Annie's. The wee man removed his sun specs and stared in disbelief. Sabastian and Hughie stared at each other and Peter burst out laughing.

Andra's was dressed from head to toe in a Mickey Mouse costume – complete with huge ears and enormous buttons holding up his short red pants.

"In the name o' the wee man!" Annie said.

"Here you keep me oot o' this," the wee man said.

"What's this, then?" the doctor asked.

"This is Doctor 654 frae the Masons," Annie said.

"Well, howdy Pardner," Andra said with outstretched hand.

"What's with the cartoon gear?" the doctor asked.

"Why, y'all, this is ma Masonic regalia, from the ole United States branch of which Ah am a brother," Andra replied proudly.

"*Never!*" the doctor said.

"But it is, honest," Andra said. "Look," he said thrusting the letter that came with it. "Look whit is says, 'you are now a fully paid-up member of the MM organisation'."

"Let me see that," Annie said, snatching the note from his hand and quickly perusing it. "MM – Mickey Mouse club, ya eejit,"she snapped.

Sabastian, who still had Andra's certificate in his hand, immediately tore it in two and let it drop to the floor, turned and left.

The wee man, lifted the drum, walked over to the wall pictures, stood to attention at King Billy's picture, snapped his heels and saluted smartly. He stepped to the side, faced the Pope and banged the drum twice as hard as he could, turned and, without a word, left taking the bass drum with him.

The doctor merely shook his head, patted Andra sympathetically on the shoulder and exited.

Andra stood, his chin hitting the ground. His dream day had become a nightmare.

Annie felt sorry for Andra. She knew how much it all meant to him and kissing him affectionately on the cheek, she said, "Don't worry, Andra, everythin' will turn oot a'right."

Andra did not look up. Nothing would be all right. Hadn't everything collapsed all around him? All at once the Lodge, the Supporters' Club, the Masons, each of them had all abandoned him in one go.His life had exploded. There was nothing left. Andra felt sorry for himself. He looked up at his favourite picture. "How could *you* let this happen tae me?" he cried. "Ah've always stuck up for *you* – banged the drum harder passin' Celtic Park an' that."

Annie turned to Peter. "Looks like yer prayers in the chapel fell oan deaf ears, son," she said.

"Ah don't believe they did," Peter said. "Ah distinctly heard a voice say that my dad's troubles would soon be over."

"You hear a' the wrang things Peter. If ye hadnae listened tae yer maw ye'd be a plumber by noo," Andra said with bitterness.

"Ach well he'll soon be flushin' sins away," Hughie said cheerily.

"You shut yer face," Andra said, "or Ah'll be chokin' *your* pipes."

"Ah won't accept that my prayers were rejected," Peter said.

"Ma prayers are always rejected," Andra said.

"What makes ye say that?" Peter asked.

"Twelve-nothin'," Andra replied dejectedly.

Peter laughed. "Never mind Dad," he said, "*He* must have something else in mind for you."

"Aye, well Ah widnae be surprised that He's got somethin' else in mind for me. He's got it in for me, that's for sure. No' only does he take a' ma dreams aff me but he sticks a cannibal in next door."

"Wullie is nae cannibal," Annie snapped. "It's you that's blinkered. Maybe if ye took they blinkers aff *He* would've sorted things oot for ye."

"Ah am nut blinkered." Andra said, hurt at the suggestion. "But, if ye ask me Ah think that Al Jolson there is a witch doactor. Nothin's went right since he showed up. Ah think he's put a spell oan me."

"Don't talk rubbish, Dad," Peter said. "Wullie is one of the nicest, most tolerant men it's been my privilege tae meet. He is not one bit prejudiced. In fact he told me he was a Catholic having been converted by a Franciscan missionary."

"A Catholic, eh?" Andra's eyebrows came down."Ah knew there was somethin' aboot him. Ah should've known when he walked past that picture o' the Pope he bowed doon and made the sign o' the cross. Ah thought he had hurt his knee and was scratchin' his heid. Ah should've known better, so Ah should."

"Aye, it was one of my order that converted him, a Franciscan," Peter said proudly.

"And he lived tae tell the tale?" Andra said. "Zulu coupon in there didnae stick him in a pot and throw an Oxo in as well?"

"Och, stoap this nonsense," Annie blurted out. "We're lucky tae hiv such a nice quiet man next door. We could easily have had a ned."

"Well, Ah still say Scotland for the Scots. He should be sent back tae where was born."

"He was born in the Third World," Peter reminded him.

"Ah don't care if he was born in Disneyworld," Andra said.

"You look mair like *you* were born in Disneyworld," Annie said, tweaking his Mickey Mouse ear.

"Ach, away and make some tea," Andra said.

"Want a piece oan cheese?" Annie said, adding to his embarrassment.

"Ach, away ye go," Andra said, taking a playful swipe at her. Annie retreated to the kitchen.

"It's good for ye," Hughie said.

"Whit is?" Andra asked.

"Cheese," Hughie said. "Ma maw said it was good for yer eyes."

"Aye, well you're gonny hiv two black wans in a minute if ye don't shut yer trap," Andra threatened.

"It's *you* that wull have tae be careful o' traps, "Annie laughed, popping her head round the kitchen door.

"Very funny!" Andra said, adding, "Peter, away you in there and get Al Jolson in here. Ah want that spell lifted."

"Ye're not serious, Dad," Peter protested.

"Ah'm dead serious," Andra sniped. "That yin is intae voodoo as well as eatin' people, Ah'm tellin' ye."

"Whit's voodoo, Andra?" Hughie asked.

"A wee doll is made o' ye an' they stick pins intae it." Andra said.

"Jist like wulks?" Hughie said, amazed.

"Aye, just like wulks – then they eat ye."

"And you think Wullie is stickin' pins in you and has put a spell on ye?" Hughie said in disbelief.

"There's nae other explanation," Andra said.

"Whit makes ye think he's been stickin' pins intae ye Andra?" Hughie wondered.

"Ah took a drink o' watter this moarnin' and became a human sprinkler – comin' oot everywhere, so it was," Andra said.

"Whit did ye dae?"

"Ah hurried oot tae the verandah and watered the windae boax," Andra said.

"Noo, stop this," Peter said angrily.

"Away and get him, Peter," Andra argued. "Ah want that spell lifted."

"Ah'll go in and see him," Peter said, heading for the door.

"Drag him in if ye hiv tae," Andra called after him.

Peter was gone only a few minutes and returned alone.

"Where is he?" Andra snapped.

"He's lyin' doon." Peter said, "Don't forget he's got a bad heart."

"He's got nae heart," Andra said. "*Everythings* went wrang in ma life the minute Ah first clapped eyes oan him, so it has."

"Aye, well, everythin' went wrang in *ma* life the first time Ah clapped eyes oan *you*," Annie said, entering with a tray.

113

"Ach, ye don't mean that, Annie," Andra was hurt. "Ah gave ye everything."

Aye, maistly the boak," Annie said.

"Oh! Whit boak was that, Annie? Hughie said. "Ah read wan wan time. It was aboot a wee widden boy who, when he telt a lie, his nose got bigger."

"Ah didnae know they'd written a book aboot Andra," Annie said, "Wis it a blue nose?"

"It was a widden nose," Hughie said.

"Aye, that could be Andra," Annie said, "A widden nose goes wi' a widden heid."

"Well, Ah don't care whit youse say," Andra went on, "Cannibals an' witch doactors shouldnae be allowed intae these Glesca high flats."

"Ah suppose you would hiv them build mud huts roon the Green?" Annie snapped.

"Better still, Celtic Park," Andra said.

"Right!" Peter said, "Ah'll away in again but if Wullie is still lyin' doon Ah'm not goin' to waken him."

"Jist you get him in here," Andra ordered. "And if ye find any wee dolls wi' pins stuck in them, bring them in as well. Two can play at that gemme. Annie see if ye can find that gollywog oor Jean had when she was a wee lassie – and bring yer pin cushion."

"Away ye go, ya racist," Annie replied angrily.

Peter left.

"You should be ashamed o' yersel'," Annie added.

"Ah have nothin' for tae be ashamed o'," Andra argued. "Ah am merely lookin' efter ma interests and the interests of everybody up this close – *and* Glesca as well."

"Ach away, Wullie is here and while he's here he is as much a Scot as you," Annie said."Don't forget his faither was a Scottish sojer."

"Ur ye blind wumman?" Andra said, raising his voice. "*He* is frae the jungle. His faither was never seen again. They probably made a haggis oot o' him."

"Ah think you came oot the jungle," Annie replied, "ye act like an animal."

"Aye, a lion," Andra said, puffing out his chest.

"Ah think ye're mair like a monkey, Andra," Hughie said

seriously.

"*Whit?*" Andra cried, grabbing him by the throat.

"Swingin'. Know whit Ah mean," Hughie gasped.

"Oh! Aye – er – well, that's a'right then," Andra stammered.

Peter entered, once more on his own.

"Where is he?" Andra snapped.

"Ah'm afraid Wullie has gone," Peter said.

"Gone where?" Andra asked, narrowing his eyes.

"To higher places," Peter said.

"This is the tap flair," Andra said, still not getting Peter's meaning.

"Is he up in the loft?" Hughie asked.

"He's gone – he's dead," Peter said, crossing himself.

"He canny dae that tae me," Andra cried. "Ah hivnae stuck wan pin in him yet."

"Ah think seeing that ghost was too much for him. He had a heart attack," Peter added, sadly.

"Hey, maybe *he* did answer yer prayers, Peter, eh?" Andra said, sounding pleased.

"You be quiet," Annie cried, "hiv you nae respect for the deid?"

"Ah said a prayer ower him mammy," Peter said.

"That was nice, son," Annie said, dabbing her eyes. "Poor Wullie! Bronwyn hivin' tae bring up they wee boys, Osama and Saddam, by hersel'."

"They wull never come tae much," Andra said. "A boy needs a faither."

"Ah never had a faither," Hughie said sadly.

"And look how you turned oot," Andra said with sarcasm. "A wee poisoned dwarf."

"You've a cheek," Annie said angrily, "Hughie has been a faithful freen tae you. You are just delighted that Wullie has gone because he's a neighbour you didnae approve of a *black* neighbour."

"That's no' true," Andra said.

"Then, whit *is* the reason?" Annie asked, hands on hips.

"Because he's wan o' your crowd – that's another wan less in this world."

"You'll answer for your attitude one day, Dad," Peter said.

"So wull you – and your flight frae the faith," Andra replied.

"Ye hivnae left Wullie in there wi' Bronwyn and they boys, hiv ye?" Annie asked, worriedly.

"There's nobody in," Peter said.

"She's probably away doon tae the benefits oaffice," Andra said.

Annie scowled at him. "She'll get a shock when she comes back," Annie said,

"Ach, he hadnae long tae go anyway," Andra snorted.

"Whit makes ye think that, Andra?" Hughie asked.

"Ah was gonny chuck him ower the balcony," Andra said,

"Don't talk nonsense," Annie said. "A minute ago ye were talkin' aboot stickin' pins in him."

"Ye know," Peter interrupted, "Ah just don't understand it. Ah definitely came away frae chapel with the distinct impression that my prayers had been heard – that my dad's troubles would be taken away from him – Ah heard that voice."

"Well, that only goes for tae prove ma point. When ye start hearin' voices in yer heid you ur definitely insane. Ah've been sayin' that a' alang." Andra said, pleased with himself.

"So ye hiv, Andra, Ah heard ye," Hughie agreed.

"Ye canny hurry God," Annie said, "*He* does things in his ain time."

"Maybe *He*'s busy," Hughie said.

"Busy daein' whit?" Andra asked. "He has heard o' ma troubles but has done nothin'. Me a true and faithful servant, tae."

"Ah didnae know you were a servant, Andra," Hughie said, surprised. "Ur ye a butler?"

"Naw, a footman, Hughie, jist waitin' tae gie ye it right in the arse."

"Maybe *He* wants for tae help ye, Andra, but disnae recognise ye sittin' there like Mickey Mouse."

"Ah feel let doon," Andra said, "Ah feel ridiculous."

"So ye should," Annie said. "If ye were gonny look like a Disney character ye should've looked like Goofy."

"Ah must've replied tae the advert underneath the Masons wan, that's the only explanation," Andra said shaking his head. He stood in front of the king and looked him straight in the eye. "You should've helped me," he moaned. "A' ma life Ah've been good tae ye, never forgot Christmas, battered the drum as hard as Ah could passin' a nun in the street. Tried tae get the Pope tae join us. Where wur you when Ah was lookin' at that magazine?"

"Ah'm no' Specsavers, ye know." A voice said. Andra jumped back.

"Did youse hear that?" he cried in jubilation.

"Hear whit?" Annie asked.

"The King, he spoke tae me," Andra said, hardly able to contain himself.

"Oor Wullie spoke tae ye?" Annie hid a smile.

"He did," Andra cried.

"Whit did he say?"

"He said he wisnae Specsavers," Andra said.

"It's no' glesses ye need Andra," Annie said, "it's a hearin' aid."

"Aye, Ah never heard a thing as well," Hughie said.

"Ye're hearin' things," Annie said, "And ye know whit ye're efter sayin' aboot folk who hear voices in their heid."

Andra pointed a shaking finger at Peter.

"It's him, int it?" he said, "He is contagious – his voices are leapin' frae his heid tae ma heid."

"Maybe God just sounds like King Billy," Hughie said.

"Ah heard him and naebody wull tell me otherwise," Andra was adamant.

"Drink yer tea," Annie said, pushing a cup across the table.

"No' tea, hen," Andra said. "Somethin' stronger, Ah think." He retrieved a bottle from the sideboard and Hughie smiled broadly.

A sudden storm began to howl and rain lashed against the window.

"Oh, Ah think *He* must have heard ye, Andra," Annie said, "better watch yersel'."

"Ah'm frightened o' naebody," Andra said with bravado. "In fact Ah think Ah'll gie *Him* a piece o' ma mind."

Andra pulled open the door and stepped out on to the balcony. He stood erect, looking up into the sky with the lashing rain stinging his face and the strong wind howling in his ear.

"Andra, come in here at wance," Annie called. "Look at the weather – get in here or ye'll catch yer death – *Andra!*"

But Andra ignored his wife's concern. Clenching his fist, he raised it towards the sky. "Ah'm no' frightened o' you," he bawled, his voice being lost in the wind. "Ye've got Sabu next door and ye're welcome tae him. But whit herm did Ah dae ye, eh? Ah hiv always been a good an' true proddy and look at the thanks Ah get."

Lightning struck down and it only made Andra more determined. "Make as much noise as ye like but you an' me are finished – hear me?"

A swirling gust swept across the verandah, lifting Andra off his feet and carrying him over the railings. Andra screamed as he plunged down – down –

CHAPTER SEVEN

"PETER, AWAY AND GET YER FAITHER IN OR HE'LL CATCH pneumonia," Annie said, worriedly. Peter fought against the wind as he opened the door of the balcony. A few seconds later he struggled back into the house. "He's gone!" he said, stunned.

"Gone where?" Hughie asked.

"Over the top," Peter said, his voice catching.

"Whit did he dae that for?" Hughie said, "It's a terrible night."

"Oh shut up, Hughie," Annie said, her hand coming to her mouth. She fought her way on to the balcony in the hope it was not true. The wind almost blowing her off her feet. She hung on to the railings and peered over the top to the concrete twenty-seven floors below but could see nothing.

Peter came to her side and, putting an arm round her shoulder, steered his mother back into the safety of the house.

Annie flopped on to the settee and wept uncontrollably. Peter sat beside her, his arm around her, comforting her.

"Oh, Peter," she wept. "Ma Andra – he had his faults but we a' hiv oor faults. But he didnae hiv tae go like this – gone with the wind – run doon, son and see if he's a'right."

"It's twenty-seven floors, Mum," Peter said, giving no hope.

"Ah'll come doon wi' ye," Hughie said and they both left Annie weeping.

The wind had died down dramatically and Annie, once more, ventured out on o the verandah. She peered over the top of the railings but could see nothing.

Then Hughie's voice bellowed up. "Annie – Annie –"

"Aye, Hughie?" she called with hope in her voice. Maybe by some freak accident Andra's fall had been broken by some obstacle – or even divine intervention. Annie was a believer in miracles and had even gone as a prilgrim with the church to Lourdes, in France – the home of divine miracles.

"Whi – whi – whit is it, Hughie," she yelled down.

"Gonny throw us doon a scraper," Hughie answered.

"Never mind," Peter yelled. "The lift's here, we'll come up."

Seconds later the two men stumbled into the house.

"Dae ye think God was angry wi' yer Faither, there, Peter?" Annie asked trembling. She did not want to think that Andra would spend his eternal life in a place she did not want to contemplate.

Peter shook his head. "Nope, God's not nasty like that," he said. "It was the weather that was nasty – poor Dad!"

"Oh, Ah hope ye're right, son,"Annie said. "He wisnae a bad man, yer dad, just a bit over zealous. We had oor quarrels but so does every married couple. Maybe he'll be a'right."

"He canny be a'right, Annie, he's deid," Hughie said tactlessly.

"Oh!" Annie wailed and Peter scowled.

"It would be quick, mammy," Peter said.

"So it wid,"Hughie agreed."He landed right oan tap o' that big blonde's Saint Bernard dug. She's noo got a chihuahua."

"Well, *He* did say that he'd take my dad's troubles away from him – and ye couldnae take them any further away than that, eh?" Peter said, glad that he hadn't imagined the heavenly voice.

"Andra wull be at peace noo, Annie," Hughie said by way of comforting his pal's widow, "He's no' got a cannonball livin' next door tae worry aboot and he knows he'll no' get ate."

"Oh Hughie, grow up," Annie said.

"Let us pray," Peter said.

The three of them stood, heads bowed and Peter began, "Heavenly Father, take our Andra to Yourself and give him your piece, Amen."

"And make sure it's butter oan it and no' margarine 'cos he disnae like margerine Amen," Hughie added

* * *

Andra's funeral was one he would have been proud of. He had asked to be placed in an orange box and his wish to be buried in Ibrox Park be honoured.

The wee man led the cortège, banging the drum all the way to the iron gates of Ibrox and Sabastian had draped the flat-pack coffin – purchased from MFI– with Andra's blue and white scarf, his tile hat placed on top.

Sabastian had reckoned that, now that Andra had expired, it would not be right to keep up the animosity.

One of the senior Rangers directors met them at the gate and with a stern "*NO!*" barred, them from entering.

"This is not allowed for hygienic reasons," he said. "But, as he was once a supporter and self-appointed bard of the club – *and* we were bombarded by his poems, the board feels that we should send him off with an appreciative ode written in his own inimitable style. He produced a piece of paper, cleared his throat and began to read

> Staunin' here beside yoor hearse,
> I thought that I should say a verse,
> We at Scotland's greatest club,
> Are glad at last you've shut your gub.

The wee man gave the drum a final wallop as they turned away. Sabastian was disappointed at not gaining entry to the hallowed turf – just to be there.

Annie and Peter were glad that Andra would be laid to rest in a 'normal' cemetery otherwise they could never visit his grave. Peter would never remove his clerical collar and he didn't think that would go unnoticed on the terraces of Ibrox Park. Annie had asked her parish priest if Andra could be buried from the church, the Catholic tradition being that the deceased lay in the chapel overnight and, after a requiem mass, be taken for burial next morning. Annie, being a devout parishioner, the priest agreed and the cortège turned back and headed for the church where Andra was laid on two trestles. That night the roof fell in and Andra was hastily hurried on to the hearse and whisked away as fast as possible next morning.

Annie placed a bouquet of orange lilies on the grave, said a silent prayer and went home. The other mourners headed for McDougall's to drink Andra's health.

★   ★   ★

As Andra crashed over the railings that fateful night he saw the ground come up to meet him. He felt nothing on impact and only heard the yelp of Bella's dog. Suddenly he was flying through a long tunnel towards a dazzling light. Emerging, he stood up, felt himself all over and dusted himself down. He wondered about the weight on his back and twisted his arm around only to grasp a handful of feathers. Wings!

Andra had wings. "Always wanted tae be a winger," he thought with a smile.

In front of him was a golden door with the sign "Heaven - Passport control".

"This way please," a voice said.

Andra entered and, sitting behind a mother-of-pearl desk sat a white bearded man, a silver quill in his hand.

"Come away in," he said and pointed to a purple-velour cushioned chair, "sit down."

Andra sat and let his eyes scan his surroundings. Beaming cherubs flew about and reminded him of the seagulls in Rothesay.

"Now," Beardy said, "let's see – you are Andrew –"

"*Andra!*" Andra corrected, not letting him finish.

"Er yes, Andra Thomson, from Glasgow?"

"Glesca," Andra said.

"Er, yes Glesca," Beardy said.

"Look," Andra snapped, "Ah want ta know whit Ah'm daein here? Wan minute Ah'm oot oan ma ain verandah hivin' words wi' your boss and the next Ah'm landin' oan tap o'a big dug."

"You just belt up," Beardy said. "We know all about your chat wi' the High Heid yin. Now, do you know who I am?"

"Santy Claus?" Andra asked.

"This is the Gateway to Heaven and I am Peter," Beardy said.

"Ma son, who is temporarily insane, is called efter you," Andra said.

"You have caused quite a stir during your time on earth," Beardy said, perusing some official looking papers.

"Ah've jist been a good Proddy," Andra said.

"We don't have Proddies up here," Beardy said, "*Or* Catholics, Muslims, Hindus, Jews, Buddhists or anything else – we just have *people*. Now, looking at your record, you seem to have been a bigot and a racist – and that is intolerable."

"Hey, wait a minute," Andra cried, "A' them people provoked me. Ah am nut a bigot – they are the bigots. They claim that they are the chosen people when it's a well known fact that *we* arra people."

"*Everybody* is the People," Beardy said. "You have heard the expression, Jock Tamson's Bairns? – well that means exactly what it says. We are all equal in the eyes of our Heavenly Father. Your attitude in Rome was dreadful. You complained about it at every turn – you mocked the Holy Father."

"Ah thought he was the windae cleaner," Andra protested.

"Listen, you," Beardy said, pointing to a trap door on the floor. "See that trap door?" he said. "Well, that's the road to hell." He lifted the door and a ten foot flame shot up with a stench of sulpher smoke. "You know what hell is, don't you?" he asked, closing the door.

Andra nodded. "Aye, twelve-nothin'," he said.

"Well, unless you are willing to turn over a new leaf and promise never to be bigoted or racist again, it's through that trap door you will go."

"Well, could ye tell me, hiv ye any good pubs up here?" Andra felt parched.

"*We* have many with live – er – dead entertainment *and* a Happy Hour is *every* hour – all drinks are free."

"Ah'm impressed – whit aboot fitba'?" he asked.

"Very popular, up here," Beardy said. "We have a Rangers and a Celtic team. Rangers win *every* game they play."

"Aw, this *is* heaven, right enough!" Andra cried.

"Yes, they take it week about. Rangers win one week and Celtic the next. We like to keep their earthly fans happy," Beardy said.

"Ach, ye jist spoilt it there," Andra grumbled. "Whit aboot music? Will Ah be able for tae play the pianna up here?"

"Great music here," Beardy said, "All the great composers – Mozart, Beethoven – we have them all – *and* you will be able to play the piano – although you'll be more likely be involved with the harp."

"That suits me," Andra said.

"You play it?" Beardy asked, surprised.

"Ah drink it," Andra said.

"Now, there's one thing I must make clear to you," Beardy said. "You will recall that in the Good Book it says, 'In my Father's kingdom there are many mansions'."

"Of coorse Ah remember that," Andra said. "Imagine askin' me a question like that dae Ah remember?"

"Yes, well we used to house every newcomer in their own

mansion but, alas, we have run out of mansions and now everybody has to double up in a luxury furnished flat. Yours overlooks a beautiful pea green sea."

"*Whit?*" Andra cried.

"All right, how about a cobalt-blue sea?"

"Aye, that's better, "Andra sighed. "Don't frighten me like that again."

"And, you will want to meet your flatmate?"

"Sure," Andra said.

Beardy flicked on the intercom.

"Gabriel," he said, "Send in Andrew – er – Andra Thomson's flatmate."

Wullie walked in beaming all over.

"Aw, naw!"Andra bawled. "No' him – no' him. Ah jist got rid o' him."

"Very well," Beardy said and flicked on the intercom once more. "Gabe," he said, "Send in number 252 – Mr Thomson still hasn't lost his earthly bigoted ways, it would seem."

"Your new flatmate," Beardy said pointing to the golden door.

Andra stood up and collapsed as a smiling Pope Pius the Sixth entered with outstretched arms. He wore the pure white garb that Andra saw the pontiff wear in Rome.

"*Il Mio Figlio,*" he said and, being in heaven, where all know-ledge is given, Andra understood it to mean, "My Son!"

Andra went berserk. He fell on to his knees and frantically tugged at the ring pull on the trap door of Hell – but it would not budge. Clenching his fists, he began to batter at it – bawling:

"*NICK* – hey *NICK* – open up *NICK* – for God's sake, *NICK* – open up wull ye —"

THE END

Lindsay Publications

PO Box 812 Glasgow G14 9NP
Tel/Fax 0141 569 6090
ISBN Prefix 1 898169